Schlock! Bi-

Schlock! Bi-monthly Vol. 2 Issue 2 – December/January 2013/14

Editor: Gavin Chappell. Published by Horrified Press (horrifiedpress.wordpress.com/)

CONTENTS

Welcome to the second issue – *k! Bi-Monthly*, containing more of the best stories to have been published in *Schlock! Webzine* (www.schlock.co.uk) and its anthologies.

There's been some debate about precisely what Bi-Monthly means, and brief research uncovered the unhelpful fact that the phrase can mean either twice a month or every two months. For the purpose of this magazine, we're taking it to mean the latter. Hope that dispels any confusion.

We're also proud to announce the publication of three new Schlock! anthologies, like this magazine containing some of the best stories to feature in the webzine. Hence the titles: *The Year's Best Schlock! Horror, The Year's Best Schlock! Sci-fi* and *The Year's Best Schlock! Fantasy*. All available in print and eBook formats from Amazon.com

Meanwhile, in this edition, we have another installment of Gregory KH Bryant's planetary romance, *The Caves of Mars*; another *Uncle Tickle* strip; a horror story of sin and suffering from Jason Osmond entitled *John Brown*; a historical swords-and-sorcery blood and thunder oriental fantasy by Damir Salkovic called *In The Gates of the Inner City*; and my own sword and soul novella, *The House of Skulls*.

None of them particularly Christmassy in theme, but have a Happy Yuletide all the same! See you in the New Year!

-Gavin Chappell

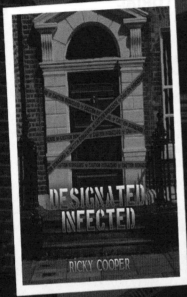

UNDEAD LIVING

Horror master Thomas M. Malafarina brings you this compilation of short stories about the undead in comtemporary settings. Included in this volume: Feeding Frenzy - Michael Collins, The Supreme Race - Catherine Jordan, The Storm - Kristina Mosley, The Collectors - Fallon Stoeffler, Trouble With The Tooth Fairy - Victoria Rowe, Angel Of Mercy - Joseph Rubas, Night Drive - C. Inferno, Encounter In The Dead Of Night··· - Sergio Palumbo, Kittens With Chainsaws - Johannes Pinter, Even The Great Will Fall - Thomas M. Malafarina, Handsome Jack - C. M. Saunders, Richard The Vampire - Joshua Malbin, Responsibility - Paul Stansfield, The Benefits of Being Dead - Benjamin Blake, The Price Of Rice - Mark Slade.

FALLEN STONES

When Stephanie Wright and her family inherit and move into a luxuriously renovated rural Schuylkill County farmette she believes all of her worries are over. But then her husband, Jason stumbles on a small ancient family burial site on the property. He decides to destroy the headstones, keeping the gravesite a secret so not to spoil his wife's newfound happiness. But sometimes the dead have their own agenda. When Stephanie begins researching her family genealogy she uncovers a terrible family tragedy, the true unholy reason for what they originally perceived as good fortune rears it hideous head. The story has plenty of suspense, supernatural intrigue, and down and out gut wrenching terror to keep any reader, horror fan or not flipping pages and hungry for more.

GHOST SHADOWS

Like a dark cloud of foreboding, stories of horror can cast their ghostly silhouettes across our very souls. Ghost Shadows is a collection of thirteen such stories by modern day master of the macabre, Thomas M. Malafarina. From tales of psychological terror to those involving the demonic tortures of Hell itself, Malafarina seeks to cast his own ghost shadows across the souls of his legion of devoted readers.

AVAILABLE FROM AMAZON.COM

Thomas M. Malafarina (www.ThomasMMalafarina.com) is an author of horror fiction from Berks County, Pennsylvania. To date he has published four horror novels "Ninety-Nine Souls", "Burn Phone", "Eye Contact" and "Fallen Stones" as well as five collections of horror short stories; "Thirteen Nasty Endings", "Gallery Of Horror", "Malafarina Maleficarum Vol. 1", Malafarina Maleficarum Vol. 2", "Ghost Shadows" and most recently "Undead Living". He has also published a book of often strange single panel cartoons called "Yes I Smelled It Too; Cartoons For The Slightly Off Center". All of his books have been published through Sunbury Press. (www.Sunburypress.com).

In addition, many of Thomas's works have appeared in dozens of short story Anthologies and e-magazines. Some have also been produced and presented for internet podcasts as well. Thomas is best known for the twists and surprises in his stories and his descriptive often gory passages have given him the reputation of being one who paints with words. Thomas is also an artist, musician, singer and songwriter.

JOHN BROWN   *Jason Osmond*

JOHN BROWN unzipped his fly, situated himself in front of the urinal, and dropped his fat, hairy dick. *Asparagus*, he thought, cringing at the smell. *Makes it stink so bad.*

He was alone.

The restroom was a dimly lit, disease infested hole-in-the-wall, located next to a New York subway station, deep underground. It was a long, concrete rectangle with four stalls, three urinals, two sinks, and one massive mirror—all of which were jammed up together along the right side of the room.

For many obvious reasons, John avoided public restrooms. But at three in the morning, when he knew his tiny bladder wouldn't make it home to his high-rise loft, he had no choice but to use it.

When he finished, he zipped up, and eyed the sinks. But he decided against washing his hands. Instead, he examined himself in the mirror. *You are one handsome son of a gun,* he thought, with a wink, a point, and a click of the tongue. With jet-black hair cut to perfection, tan skin, and body like a Roman God—John Brown knew he had it all.

Then, in the mirror, he saw a man in rags, sitting in the corner of the room, across from the restroom door. He spun around, but found no one. He looked back in the mirror—again, no one. The only thing in the corner was a dark, oily stain on the ground.

John loosened his tie, and stared at the corner for longer than he knew he should have. He was a little drunk, he knew, but not drunk enough to be seeing things, or so he thought. He rubbed his eyes, walked to the corner, and waved his shoe over the stain, proving to himself that there was truly nothing there.

And then he remembered.

He looked at his watch. It was exactly a year ago today that he'd stopped by to use this same restroom. He recalled the date easily because it was the same day he lost the Truman account, and was almost fired for it—a day he'd never forget. And to celebrate his failure, he got wasted, (more smashed than usual) found himself in a bar fight on 54th, rented a hooker, got himself a room at the Four Seasons just for fun, and then somehow ended up here on his way home—same place, almost at the same time, too if his memory was correct. Only then, a man had been sitting in that corner, a man that John Brown could never forget, a man he swear he just saw.

John didn't notice the man as he walked into the restroom, exactly one year ago. He just passed him by on the way to the urinals like he would a discarded piece of trash. While he was relieving himself, he tilted his head back, and drank the last drops of a single serving sized bottle of vodka. And that's when he saw the bum in the mirror, out of the corner of his eye.

John grunted. He had always disliked the poor, and the homeless. For the same ambiguous reason he hated cockroaches.

The bum had black scraggly hair, cut short. John assumed he was bit older than he was—thirty, forty maybe. He had on torn up dress slacks, equally torn up leather shoes, and a green button down shirt. He gave the appearance of a once wealthy man who had failed in life. But the thing that stood out most to John was a ring on the man's middle finger. It was massive, gold, and laced with diamonds —so beautiful.

John thought for a moment, then put the tiny, empty vodka bottle under his urine stream. Carefully, he filled it up. After he was done, and zipped, he recapped the bottle, and walked over to the man.

John sniffed. The man smelt like a dead animal carcass covered in crap. He covered his nose with his tie and held out the little bottle. "Trade you some alcohol for that ring," he said.

The man, whose head had been tilted forward the whole time, looked up at him. John took a few steps back. The man's eye sockets were nothing more than gaping holes. There were scratch marks all over his face, and his skin was pallid, sweaty, and infected with acne. His hands were bloated and decaying. His lips were thin, and cracked in more places than John cared to count. But the most disturbing thing for John was the man's teeth. They were perfect, beautiful—almost as nice as his teeth were.

The decrepit man gasped, as if John's voice had shocked him.

John cringed, then decided against the ring. He tossed the bottle of piss into the man's lap, and left without another word.

A year later, exactly, the man was gone, but a stain remained.

John snorted at the stain. Then he grabbed the restroom door handle and gave it a tug. Then he gave it another tug. He put both hands on the handle and pulled as hard as he could, but it didn't move. He kicked at it, kicked again—yanked—but nothing. He let out a litany of curses, all of them from A to Z, in every combination possible, as he yanked some more. After a few minutes, he gave up. In his fury, John took hold of the trashcan that was next to the stain, and tossed it against the door, spilling its contents all over. He was flushed red and sweating.

For a moment, John just seethed in his frustration, panting. Hunched over, with his hands on his knees, he glanced down at the stalls. Maybe there was another exit? He ran down to the other end—nothing. He roared, then kicked one of the stalls in. The door swung open, recoiled, and slammed shut again. He searched the walls and ceiling for a possible air vent, but none were to be found. The room was solid cinderblock, all the way around.

He made his way back to the restroom entrance, hitting, and kicking things along the way. His only link to the outside world, and most likely his only source for air, was a two inch crack under the door.

He never would have imagined himself in this position, crouching down on all fours, peeking out into the dimly lit subway station in the waking hours of the early morning. "Help!" he shouted. "Hey! Anyone out there? Hello? Anyone? Can you hear me? Anyone!" He slapped his palm on the door a few times. He could only imagine how ridicules he looked.

He was about to give up when a pair of pink stilettos walked by. He started shouting again, banging on the door, frantically. But it wasn't until he yelled out "Please!" that she, or he, (you never know) finally stopped. For a moment, the high heels stood in place, not moving, facing away from him. He assumed the person was looking around for his voice. "Over here, the restrooms!" he shouted, but shoes stood still. "Hey, did you hear me?" he yelled. "You, in the pink shoes, please, can you help me? I'm locked in, somehow, here, in the restroo—can you turn around, please? I'm over here!" He pounded on the door.

The shoes turned around, and when they did, John Brown's eyebrows lowered, for he found them strangely familiar. Something about how the toes came to a point, how the straps laced up the ankles—he'd seen those heels before. "Yes! This way. Over here. The men's room. Thank you."

The stilettos walked towards him, slowly, hesitantly. He noticed this apprehensiveness in their step and spoke to reassure the person: "Don't worry, it's not a trick," he said. "No one's going to hurt you, either." He tried to laugh. "I just need your help. Can you see if you can somehow unlock…or, or un-jam it? Or better yet, do you have a phone? Can you slip it down here so I can make a call? Or maybe you can call! Yes, call 911, or— hello? Can you respond so that I know that you are—?"

The high heels came to a stop, but what caught his attention was how close they were to the door. The pointed toes could not be more than an inch from the crack where his eyes were. No normal person would come that close, he knew. And there was no voice, no response.

The subway lighting outside the restroom was much brighter than inside, so the shoes cast long shadows towards John. He tried to communicate to the person again, but nothing happened. An eerie twinge of ice pricked his back and neck. He let out a confused sigh, then sat back up against the wall. After a while, he examined his watch. Three minutes passed, four— five minutes, but the shoes did not move.

He put his left hand down on the ground, and felt something warm on the cement. When he lifted his hand, he found it covered in grime. He let out a disgusted moan. Without realizing it, he'd parked himself exactly on that greasy stain, and had gotten what was left of that bum all over him.

His stomach lurched, and something crawled up his throat. He had no choice but to get up, run to the sink, and let it all come out (he had always been known for his weak stomach; the kids in school used to call him puke-face-Jonny). The alcohol, the B.L.T. for lunch, the baked ziti with a side of asparagus for dinner, and the Tiramisu he'd stuffed his face with that night, was now just a mess in sink. He spit a few times, then wiped his mouth with his French cuffed sleeve. But as he turned on the water to wash his hands, he felt more coming on. His face tingled under the skin. Sweat broke through every pore. He leaned forward for another hurl, but nothing came. The muscles in his torso cramped up, and pushed, but only air escaped. The third time he spasmed, he felt something hit the back of his throat. Whatever it was, it was cold, like an ice-cube—so thick and long that it made him gag. His oesophagus contracted, and forced the

6

freezing thing up and out. When it hit the sink, it made a loud, clinking noise.

With all the tears in his eyes, it was hard to make out what it was. When he could finally focus, and he'd caught his breath, he saw a pale, bloated finger, chewed off near the third knuckle with a massive, golden ring on the end of it. Its many tiny diamonds glistened in the fluorescent light.

John found himself with his back up against the wall on the opposite side of the room, with his eyes wide open. He covered his mouth with his left hand, and aimlessly felt the wall with his right as he slid down to a crouching position. He couldn't breathe, not normally anyway. Once he realized that the grime that was all over his left hand was now all over his face, he lost all strength and fell on his side. The last thing he saw before he blacked out were the bright pink stilettos still standing outside the door.

It was the smell that woke him up. The restroom had stunk before, but something had changed. This smell was a kind of tangy twinge, rank enough to wake the dead and make his eyes burn. He pulled himself up to a sitting position, blinking profusely. He tongued the inside of his mouth, and slowly stood up with a groan. Looking at his watch, he saw that he'd only been out a few minutes. When he saw that there was no puke—and no finger—in the sink, he blamed the whole episode on the alcohol, like any rational drunk would do. He must have fallen unconscious after he'd taken a piss, and dreamed the whole thing up, including the door being locked. He smiled, spit on the ground, and gave the door a good hard yank.

But the door didn't budge.

"What the—" he said, his knuckles turning white from squeezing so tight. He yanked on it again, but still, it wouldn't move. "No!" he yelled, then slapped the door. "No, no, no, no, no!" He really *was* locked in! That part, at least, he had not dreamed up.

He tossed himself down on the floor, and peered out through the crack. Like the finger, the shoes were gone. Then it hit him, where he'd seen those high heels before. The memory came back so fast and so hard that he could almost feel it rattle around on the inside of his skull. It was the same night, exactly one year ago—the same night he'd met the bum.

Amber was her name, and she was a hundred dollars an hour. He'd ordered her up, and had taken her to his rented suite at the four seasons. She was quite girl a—red hair, pale freckled skin, and couldn't be more twenty. Her face resembled that of a doll, plastic and empty, which had little to no life in it.

While he was having his way with her, he noticed that she never once smiled, or frowned, or expressed anything humanly normal. A few times, he'd jokingly checked to make sure that she was still alive. All she would do is nod and blink, nod and blink. And while he played, he affectionately called her his little red robot. But the thing he remembered most about her was a thick, protruding scar on her back that travelled down at an angle, from shoulder blade to tail bone. It was a mountain range of scare tissue that almost defined her in some dark, poetic way, and most likely had a terrible back-story, (no pun intended) and was a tale he had no interest in hearing.

After he was done with her, he sat down and picked up his wallet. When he opened it up, he found six Benjamin Franklins starring up at him, crisp and new. He grabbed a couple, hesitated, then put them back in, and closed it up. He didn't know why he decided not to pay her; he was very pleased with her performance. He just didn't feel like doing it, that was it. He had had a bad day, and he just didn't want to. He tapped his wallet on the palm of his hand a few times, and then put it in a drawer. Then he told her that he wasn't going to fork out the cash, and to get out.

She didn't move—never said a word, just stood at the door as if waiting for a punchline.

John Brown got up, grabbed her by the arm, and forced her into the hallway.

After shutting the door, and turning off the lights, he crawled back into bed, and stared at the ceiling. For about two hours he tried to sleep, but couldn't. Everything was starting to irritate him. The ticking clock on the wall, the sound of traffic down below, outside the window—but what bugged him the most was the crack under the door that glowed bright yellow from the hallway. So he took a pillow, walked over, and dropped it against the bottom of the door. As he adjusted it to cover all the light, he noticed two shadows. Someone was standing outside the door. He paused for a moment, frozen in thought. Then he stood up and looked out the peephole. No one was there. He looked down. The shadows were still there. So he got on his hands and knees, and looked out through the one inch crack. Two pink stilettos were pointing right at him.

He opened the door, slowly, then looked around. No sight of Amber, or anyone—only the heels. He found it so strange that a girl would leave her shoes like that. Maybe it was to let her pimp know where to send the collection agents? With that thought in mind, he decided to check out early, and go home. It was two-thirty three in the morning when he left the hotel.

The bathroom lights above his head flickered off, then back on again. He had finally come to the realization that he might have to stay the night in the restroom. Surely, someone would find him soon. He wondered whom he could sue for this. The city? Maybe. Or were the subways systems privately owned? He didn't know. But it would be the first thing he'd research when he got back to the office—that was for sure.

After banging on the door for what felt like another hour, he ended up sitting on the sink counter top, just sitting, staring at the stain on the ground.

The smell was getting worse by the minute. It reminded him of a bar restroom he'd started a fight in, last year on 54th Street—the same night he'd met the bum, the same night he'd had his way with Amber.

He remembered, he'd just gotten off work and decided to hit the drinks, alone. His boss had yelled at him for thirty-three minutes straight. Truman account this, and Truman account that, and how you're dead if you ever do something stupid like that ever again, blah, blah, blah—stuff like that. And after a dozen Jack Daniels, John found himself in need of immediate relief, so he waddled his way over to the restroom.

It was only a one-manned room, so he had to wait his turn. He remembered how angry he felt, waiting. No one made him wait! He watched his wristwatch tick by. Five minutes passed, then ten—fifteen minutes, and so on. And the longer he waited, the worse the stink became. Even outside the restroom, the smell was so thick and palpable, that every breath John took felt like taking a bite out of the man's own faecal waste. Whoever was inside ignored every knock, and every one of John's threats to break the door down. In retrospect, he didn't know why he didn't just leave after the first five minutes, and use a restroom somewhere else. He figured it had to do with the fact that he was a terribly angry drunk, and he wanted to teach the guy a lesson. That, and he'd finally found someone to let out all his frustration on.

When the man finally came out, John's bladder was about to explode. He was probably in his forties, overweight, balding, and hunched over. He looked terribly ill. But John was too angry to care. He shoved him up against the wall, and slugged him hard in the stomach. How was he supposed to know that the man had major constipation issues, and dangerously large gallbladder stones?

A bottle of Ex-Lax dropped out of the man's coat pocket as he fell to his knees. As he made a move to pick it up, John Brown kicked it away. Then John kneed the man in the face. This action caused a violent eruption that led to a full-out bar riot, which eventually attracted the cops, and ultimately caused John to piss his pants.

After the dust settled, and John had convinced the officers of his innocence,

he watched an ambulance carry the middle aged, overweight, balding man away. As the red and yellow flashing lights disappear into the distance, he realized how horny fighting had gotten him. So he found the number to a "highbrow" escort service, and ordered up some flesh. He told the seductive voice over the phone that he was only in town for one night, staying at the Four Seasons, and to send the best redhead they had.

Two hours had gone by and John was still trapped inside that restroom. Suddenly, he realized that he needed to defecate. It hit him with an unusual urgency. *Oh, how perfect,* he thought, but no, he wouldn't have it. He'd hold it in all night rather than use one of those nasty, disgusting stalls. He walked around in hopes that the issue would slip away, and turn into a problem he could deal with later. But after twenty minutes, the pain was too unbearable to ignore.

He threw open the closest stall and stumbled in. As he unbuckled his belt, the door slammed shut behind him. He locked it, more out of habit than anything else. Then he pulled down his drawers, sat, and let everything fly free. He hardly had time to inspect the toilet seat in his haste.

After the ride was over, John Brown let out a sigh, and rubbed his face with his right hand (the clean one). It was then that he noticed there wasn't any toilet paper. He closed his eyes and swallowed this reality hard. He hoped with every inch of his soul that the other stalls had some.

He cracked his legs open and peered down at the masterpiece he'd created. It was the worst kind: bright green diarrhoea. He looked away, ashamed with himself, and coughed a few times. As he wrapped his hand in his tie, preparing to flush, he felt something touch his dangling testicles. He froze. Slowly, he looked back down in between his legs. A smooth, white hand extended up out of the green mess, and latched on. John attempted to stand, but was pulled back down. He screamed a high pitched scream he'd never heard himself make before. The hand gave a hard yank, and John's body wrenched forward. It pulled again, this time harder, and John screamed again.

He stuck both his hands down in the bowl, and attempted to pry open the fingers. He felt his fingernails sink into the hand's skin, as the hand's nails sank into his scrotum. The skin around his crotch began to stretch and tear. The hand shook violently like a big mouth bass on a hook. Diarrhoea splashed out all over the bowl. John mounted his feet against the wall behind the toilet, and pushed. Something made a popping noise. He leaned forward, and pulled. His teeth clenched together, his face as red as a baboon's arse.

He remembered that he had a pen. He reached in his suit coat pocket, but when he found his pen, he found something else as well. He pulled out both objects. One of them was his favourite two hundred dollar Montblanc, and the other, a small bottle of Ex-lax. The hand below gave a particularly vicious yank, and John dropped the bottle. Then he began to stab at the hand, over and over with the pen. A few times, he missed the hand and jammed himself instead. Finally, the hand let go.

Like a loaded spring, John flew forward. His face made contact with the stall door, and busted through. Then he rammed head first into the concrete wall, and crumpled onto the ground in a messy heap.

For a moment, he did nothing but moan. After a bit of hard breathing, he managed to raise himself up on his elbows. He was shaking, and every few moments he'd get an electrifying burst of chills that made it extremely difficult for him to breathe. When the lights flickered off and on, he screamed again, and curled up into a ball again.

It took him a long time to do anything but stare at the toilet bowl. He tried to stand, but his legs were too wobbly. Covered in his own waste, he dragged himself across the floor with his forearms back to the restroom door. "Please," he said, sobbing, with his mouth under the door crack. "Please! Let me ou- ou- out! When the lights inside the restroom went completely dark, he started to bawl. He kept his focus on the crack, staring out at the bright, empty subway station floor. "Please! Help! So, s- s- s- someone, -ne, -ne, -ne. ANYONE!"

After a few minutes, the temperature in the restroom started rising. After two more hours alone in the dark, the room was a steaming, reeking sauna. John's body had tried to throw up a dozen more times, but there was nothing inside of him to be rid of. He had found himself in the corner of the room, constantly gaging, holding his legs tightly against his body. He kept his eyes on the light, hoping, and fearing at the same time to see someone walk towards the door.

Then he felt the water, or at least he thought it was water. In the dark, he could not tell what it was, but it was thick, full of small chunks, and smelled awful. It seeped in all around him, close to an inch high. There was a flushing sound, and he jumped. Then came another flush. He heard one of the sinks turn on, then the other. And the hot liquid started to rise around him.

A few large chunks plugged up the crack under the door. He kicked at them, desperately trying to conserve some light, but the water was coming too fast, and there were too many chunks to fight off. It only took about five minutes to entirely blot out the light.

John stood up, having received a fearful burst of energy. His legs were still shaky, but at least he had his balance. His first instinct was to try the door again, but of course, it was locked. So he splashed through the dark towards the sound of the sinks. When his hands found the knobs, he twisted frantically, but it did no good. Water kept pouring out. He attempted snapping off one of the faucets, but he couldn't break it.

The lights flickered back on, and he jumped backwards, screaming. Standing before him, was his own reflection...

He looked down. It wasn't just water, it was green diarrhoea—most likely *his* green diarrhoea. It was two, three—four inches deep now. His stomach gave another failed lurch, and keeled over.

A loud flushing-gurgling sound came from one of the stalls. He could see the green mess pouring out from each one, water-falling down out from under the stall doors. A thought came to him. He didn't know what was happening, but maybe he could clog one of them up? It

was a stupid idea, but he didn't know what else to do, and he was sick of cowering in the corner. He hesitated, clenched his fists together, then ran toward the stalls. He skipped the one that had the hand, and went for the second one over, kicking it open. He stepped inside, and carefully peeked down at the gushing bowl. There were no hands, or anything...unexplainable. Just some severely backed up sewage, or so it appeared.

He took off his Armani jacket, and shoved it into the hole. Then he took his foot and rammed it in, deeper and deeper until it stopped the flow. For a few moments, it seemed to work, then the jacket burst out like old faithful. It stuck to the ceiling for a second, then fell flat with a splash.

John backed up until he hit the wall, and the stall door closed behind him. He was exhausted. He shook his head a few times, closed his eyes, and slammed the back of his head against the wall as hard as he could. "Come on!" he yelled, then slammed the back of his head a few more times.

For a while, he just stood there, watching, waiting, until the diarrhoea had risen to his knees. He found himself lost in a misty, hopelessness, unable to move. Eventually, he made his way over the sinks, and stood up on the counter. He glanced at his watch, then glanced at it again. It was three in the morning, and the date read exactly one year ago. *How could that be?* He blinked at it a few times, then took it off, and dropped it into the rising mess.

He had nothing else to do, but watch and wait. The level of green mess rose incredibly fast, a foot every minute, he assumed. The warm vile covered the sinks, his ankles. It climbed up his pants and up to his thighs. When it got up to his chin, he started to pray, which was something he had only done a few times before as a child when his mother had made him.

The steaming hot gunk slipped into his nostrils, then into his ears. It burnt the whites of his eyes. He tried to keep his mouth close, but he couldn't help but scream one last time. But it wasn't a scream that came out, but more of a gurgling choke. And then he was under, consumed, trapped in the darkness of his own faecal matter.

He scrabbled in the thickness, churning the butter, trying to stay as close to the ceiling as he could, but ultimately, he sank. He sank down into the darkness until his feet touched the floor. His body began to convulse instinctively—contracting, and inhaling as he started the drowning process. And that's when something touched him.

He felt hands grabbing at his legs, his belt. Another set grabbed him from behind and flipped him upside down. A body slammed up against his torso, wrapped legs around his waist, and began to squeeze. More hands grabbed at his face, scratching viciously. He felt fingers slide into his mouth, his eyes sockets, tugging at his eyeballs. He could almost hear the tendons tearing as the fingers pulled them out, one by one.

John clawed at the body that was wrapped around him, and felt that it was naked. Then he felt a kiss on the lips. Whoever, or whatever it was, kissed him—and kissed him hard, encasing his mouth entirely, sticking a tongue deep inside John's throat.

One of John's fingernails cut into the person's back, creating a long gash down the person's back from shoulder blade to the tail bone. Something bit him on the neck, and he suddenly knew who it was that held him captive. And that was the last thing he knew before he felt himself die.

When came around, he was sitting in a corner. His eyes were gone, and his clothes were soaking wet. He was too tired to move, to think, to feel—so he just sat. He wondered, was he really dead? Was this hell? There was something on his finger—a ring, thick and heavy, that wasn't there before. *How did that get there?* he thought. Then he heard footsteps. At first, he hardly noticed them. Then he heard the sound of draining water. His body twitched, and his heart raced.

A few moments passed where nothing happened. Then he heard the footsteps again, this time louder and more prominent, coming towards him. When they stopped, John Brown heard a voice, a strangely familiar voice. "Trade you some alcohol for that ring," it said.

He lifted his face towards the voice, and gasped. Then he felt something warm land in his lap. But he didn't bother picking it up, for he knew exactly what it was.

ABOUT THE AUTHOR

Jason Osmond is a writer and entertainer in Branson Missouri. Jason comes from a world renowned family of entertainers. He enjoys reading Stephen King novels and watching the sun rise (at the same time). He is currently working on his debut novel.

Evacuation

A divorced 911 dispatcher, Chase McKinney, finds himself in the midst of an apocalypse. Contaminated vials of swine flu vaccination infected millions country-wide. Side effects turned those inoculated into zombies. Some fast. Some slow. Both deadly.

The military escorts Chase, his children and a small band of survivors to a re-opened internment camp. The purpose is to test non-infected humans with the hope of developing a cure for the diseased population.

What they find when they arrive at the camp is worse than their darkest fears ...

Vaccination

What if the H7N9 vaccination wasn't just a preventative measure against swine flu?

It seemed like the flu came out of nowhere and yet, in no time at all the government manufactured a vaccination. Were lab workers diligent, or could the virus itself have been man-made?

Chase McKinney works as a dispatcher at 9-1-1. Taking emergency calls, it becomes immediately obvious that the entire city is infected with the walking dead. His first goal is to reach and save his two children.

Could the walls built by the U.S.A. to keep out illegal aliens, and the fact the Mexican government could not afford to vaccinate their citizens against the flu, make the southern border the only plausible destination for safety?

AVAILABLE FROM AMAZON.COM

Phillip Tomasso is the author of 11 novels, and over 100 short stories and articles. He works full time as a Fire Dispatcher for 911, and lives in Rochester, NY, USA with his three children.

www.philliptomasso.com

IN THE GATE OF THE INNER CITY *Damir Salkovic*

1.

THE FLAT stone road wound down gradually into the valley. A serene silence permeated the late afternoon, the warm breeze laden with the scent of thousands of flowers. Amid the leafy expanse of orchards and beds in blossom, amid the white bloom of the almond-trees and the fantastic colours of exotic flowers, nestled the great city, its arched gate and soaring minarets and spires reflecting the last rays of the fading sun. A range of snow-capped mountains rose in the distance, shimmering in a blue haze.

Even from a distance she was ravishing, the fabled city; a courtesan at whose golden-slippered feet were laid treasures from all four corners of the world. Her roofs and minarets gleamed with bronze and gold; her ivory walls and winding streets were said to hold secrets darker than the night, forbidden pleasures from the blackest corners of the human soul. An abode of poets and assassins, of philosophers and thieves, of veiled houris and horned demons alike.

"Garden of Souls," said the large, burly man riding in front, his dark eyes widening to take in the sight.

"Laid open for a blaspheming mule like yourself." The old man riding behind him swiped at his broad back with his cane. Laughter rippled through the caravan; the man lashed the other riders with a fiery stare. "Fools laugh, but the one and only God hears everything."

"Come, Dawud," said a tall man of regal stature and attire. He wore a tunic threaded with gold and a green silken turban around his tall helmet, an abundance of jewels on his person. "Surely this beauty stirs even your hardened heart, for there is no city in the world whose wonders equal those of Samarkand."

"It's the poisoned apple that smells the sweetest," the old man spat. The small caravan joined the throng of men and beasts beneath the great arch of white stone: merchants with carts of silk and spices next to peasants whose backs bent under the burden of their wares, street-hawkers, rag-clad labourers, beggars ravaged by deformity and disease, courtesans and street performers. Through the crowd moved the pale green tunics of the *ahdath*, the city guard, their swords and helmets gleaming in the sunset.

"It was foolish to come here," old Dawud said, his crinkled eyes searching the crowd. "The Khan may bow and scrape before the throne of Isfahan, but treachery lies in his heart. No man has conquered Samarkand, the city born under the star of strife and rebellion. Darkness lurks beneath its gilded front; the old ways of sorcerers and fire-eaters still hold sway over the souls of men, and the names of the old gods are secretly invoked in vile prayer."

"Enough with the crowing," the black-haired warrior said with a sneer. "This from the hero of Dandanaqan, the bane of infidels who rode at the front of the Great Sultan's army into Baghdad."

"And drank wine from the jewelled sandal of the Caliph's favoured concubine," added another rider to a roar of mirth from the others.

"Fools!" The old man turned a deep scarlet; he was saved from responding by the nobleman's return.

"There is a caravansary in the

Zaghrimash quarter that came highly recommended for its discretion," he spoke to the men. "I have told the guards we are journeymen from Herat, in the city to haggle over spices with Parsee tradesmen. The authorities will pay us little heed. Tomorrow I shall go to the mosque in Zaghrimash and seek out Imam Hassan; he is faithful to the Sultan, and will be able to shed light on the rumours circulating against the Khan."

The procession turned into a narrow cobbled street that led away from the bazaar, leaving the crowded main thoroughfare behind them. Here the residences of the wealthy shone in full splendour; the white walls closed on grandiose fountains and gardens of flowering fruit-trees filled with the melodies of unseen song-birds. They passed by the crumbling walls of the *madinah*, the inner city at the centre of which lay the ruler's citadel, and soon found themselves in the opulent surroundings of Zaghrimash.

As night fell, the riders gathered around silver and brass trays laden with fragrantly spiced delicacies and honeyed wine; the archways of the upper floor of the caravansary opened on a view of the great city, the night specked with stars and the lights of thousands of oil-lamps. From a distance came the sounds of drunken carousing and song. The men ate and drank heartily, save for the Nizam, who shunned the wine, and old Dawud who sipped his tea in silence, staring at the moonlit rooftops.

"Something troubles you, Amin." Nizam turned to the man on his right side, a man of medium height whose bulk of shoulder and limb rivalled that of the burly Mahmoud. His blue eyes and golden skin contrasted the swarthiness of his companions, although he dressed in the same flowing trousers and tunic and wore his light brown hair braided in the style of a Seljuk cavalryman. "You keep glancing over your shoulder and into the night."

"We are watched." The warrior spoke the Oghuz tongue with a soft lilt. "Two men in the shadows of the alley across from the caravansary gate. Another in the courtyard, sending signals with a candle. But there is something else astir in the darkness, something stalking in the night."

"Let them watch. We will not give them cause for alarm, not yet. But ready yourself for a fight; I picked our location carefully - the six of us can defend our quarters against ten times as many foes."

"As you wish." The brown-haired man rose. "I'll stand first watch atop the staircase." He strode into the shadows cast by the flickering braziers and vanished through the broad entryway.

"Do you trust that man, Emir?" Dawud spoke in Persian, his eyes following the powerful figure.

"With my life," the nobleman replied.

"He is *ghulam*, a slave soldier." The old scholar shifted his weight on the velvet pillow. "A mercenary of the Byzantines before his capture. He's said to hail from the savage, mountainous lands in the East, untouched by the light of God's Word."

"In battle he is a match for a dozen men." Yunus, the youngest of the men, ventured to speak. "One of the finest swordsmen I've seen, second only to the Emir in skill but three times as ferocious." Mahmoud and the other soldier, Haroun, nodded their heads in silent agreement.

"It's not his fighting prowess that I doubt. If we're betrayed here, surrounded by enemies in a strange, hostile land, we are lost. The Khan can have us assassinated without fear of retribution; we have entered his city under guise."

"Put your mind at ease, Dawud." Nizam poured tea into the old man's cup. "He was the Vizier's personal bodyguard, a man trusted by the Great Sultan himself. Besides, were he plotting to take our lives, he needn't have waited for us to reach Samarkand. He'd have slain us as we slept."

"As you wish," the scholar replied. "But do something to allay an old man's fears. When we head to the mosque tomorrow, let him not come with us. Think of the Imam; he is the only *alim* in this city loyal to the Sultan. Without him our cause is lost."

"You do him injustice, scholar." The fine features of the nobleman clouded over. "Yet I can scarcely deny the request of the Great Sultan's trusted advisor. You two men," he indicated Yunus and Haroun, "will accompany Amin to the bazaar to draw the attention of the spies."

The men bowed in obedience. After the servants had cleared the remains of the supper, they retired to their quarters. The upper floor of the caravansary descended into darkness and silence. Yet sleep was slow in coming to the eyes of Nizam ibn Omar, whose restless gaze moved across the silent streets, across the walls and gardens beneath which beat the treacherous, unconquerable heart of the great city.

2.

A THICK miasma of noise hung over the great bazaar, a hellish din of haggling, shouting, heckling and cursing. The myriad smells of the marketplace filled the nostrils of the three men pushing through the raucous, malodorous crowd: the sharp scent of spices and horse dung, cooking food and camphor, the mixed aroma of man and beasts of burden. Above the clamour and fetor of the marketplace, the brass-covered minarets basked in the sunlight.

"I can feel eyes upon us," the wanderer said as they pressed through the crowd. "Let us find the silk-sellers and purchase a few trinkets, return to the caravansary."

"Leave the bartering to Yunus," said Haroun with a laugh. "He knows more about silken garments than the two of us; his gifts grace the supple hips of half the harlots in Shahdiz."

They shoved their way out of the crowd and into a meandering alley, the noise of the bazaar receding behind the brick walls of the tenements. Here the cloth and carpet merchants sat upon pillows and sipped tea, conversing in hushed murmur. With each step the tiled walls reached higher, casting a deeper shadow on the narrow street. Turn by twisting turn, the alley led further from the heart of the bazaar and into a confounding knot of crumbling walls and iron gates behind which empty stone courtyards gaped like the mouths of blind, leering idols. The men soon realized they were lost.

The warriors stared around uneasily. The vacant street had sunk into an ominous silence; even the steady drone of the beggars' cries had died down. From above came the sound

16

of closing shutters, a muffled exclamation in an unfamiliar tongue. Then they came: half a dozen figures in the gloom ahead, entering the alley through a hidden passageway. There was no mistaking their intent or the gleam of the long blades in their hands. The three men turned back, only to see more armed assailants blocking their way. Too late had they seen the carefully laid trap; the high walls offered no means of escape, penning them in like sheep in a charnel-house.

"A dozen," Haroun said, reaching for the daggers in his belt. "Swords against our knives. We are lost."

"We'll fight back to back." Amin drew his long knife. "Until we can't fight anymore."

Confident in their strength in numbers the attackers charged recklessly: hired swords who fought for coin, eager to complete their bloody task. Haroun dodged a diagonal slash aimed at his throat and attempted to close on his opponent, but the man next to him dealt him a glancing cut with the tip of his blade; the Seljuk cursed and whirled out of the way as another swordsman came at him, curved sword held low for the disembowelling strike. The man's momentum carried him forward, into the path of Yunus' knife: he crumpled to his knees, open eyes staring in disbelief at the blood gushing from his throat.

On the other side, Amin side-stepped a clumsy thrust and brought the pommel of his knife down, shattering the wrist of his attacker and sending his sword clattering across the street. With his free hand he grabbed the disarmed opponent by the neck and flung him in the way of the two oncoming attackers, slowing them long enough to retrieve the fallen sword. He parried the first strike with the knife and cut a yawning wound in the man's stomach, ducking beneath the second assailant's swing to hamstring him with a swift slice. A third attacker surged through the gap between his comrades, his sabre cutting a silvery arc through the murk of the alley; the steel bit into the wad of muscle between the wanderer's neck and shoulder. His sword cut upward, cleaving the head of the hamstrung assassin in two. Blood and specks of bone showered his face and for an instant the world took on a red hue.

Through the crimson mist he saw Haroun drive both daggers into the neck of a lumbering giant. Yunus had felled another attacker, but the remaining two had him against the wall, his knife no match for the reach of their long, curved blades. The attackers closed on the wanderer; he dodged and parried, his knife and sword painting the walls of the alley a dark scarlet.

In a matter of seconds the narrow alley had turned into a slaughterhouse, the cobblestones slick with blood. Trapped between the wall and the wild swings of his opponent, Haroun watched two attackers cut Yunus to his knees, then drive the glinting point of a blade through his chest, just below the collarbone. He dropped his guard for a split second and the assailant's blade cut into his side. Ignoring the pain, the Seljuk seized the foe's sword-arm, trapping the blade inside his body, and thrust the dagger in his other hand into the man's throat. The two men collapsed to the ground in a deadly embrace. Haroun saw Amin whirl between two opponents in a flurry of blades and cut one of them in half. Already the two men who had slain Yunus were approaching the wanderer from behind, swords poised for the lethal blow, and another assassin skirted the melee, his sword-arm hanging limply by his side, a dagger in his off hand. Haroun pushed the dead weight of the corpse away and tried to upright himself against the wall; the street went into a nauseating spin, darkness stealing across the corners of his vision.

Amin heard the warning cry and turned, stopping the advancing attackers dead in their tracks. Their nerve broken, the assassins turned and ran. The one with the broken wrist stared at the wanderer in wide-eyed terror, glancing frantically over his shoulder at the silhouette of his fleeing comrades vanishing into the shadows of the alley.

Bathed in blood and unarmed, the wanderer approached the remaining foe; there was nowhere to run. Two powerful hands seized the assassin by the throat. He gazed into the cold blue eyes of the stranger he'd tried to kill.

"Mercy," the assassin said. The knife fell from his numb hand as the grip on his neck grew tighter.

"Allah is merciful," the stranger replied and dashed his brains out against the wall of the alley. The assassin's body trembled for a moment, then went still.

3.

"DEATH FOLLOWS our footsteps," spoke Nizam. The washed and shrouded bodies of the slain men - the youth Yunus and all five servants - lay in the centre of the room, prepared for the burial prayer. "The Imam is dead, murdered by thieves who sacked the mosque in a riot a fortnight ago. Now this."

"Yunus died well, bringing death to your enemies." Amin's voice ran thick with fury. "As for the servants, we found them strangled upon our return. The assassins slew the stable-boy and two of the caravansary men. The master and his family barely escaped with their lives."

"Did their bloody work and vanished like spirits." The nobleman ran his fingers through his well-trimmed beard. "Soon they will return for us, either the assassins or the Khan's guard."

"Then let us bring the fight to our enemies." Mahmoud's eyes blazed. "We'll storm the Khan's palace and cut his treacherous heart out."

"It's not men we should be afraid of." Old Dawud stood by the balcony, staring into the night. "But a foulness from the deepest pits of the Abyss, the nether realms that lie outside the reaches of space."

"You spoke to the younger muezzins at the mosque, scholar. Did the Imam leave word for us?"

"We came here suspecting the Khan of plotting to overthrow the rule of the Sultan with the help of our enemies. Yet even the loathsome Ismailis, those disciples of the aberrant faith, shudder at the mention of those who worship the dread entities of the nether realms. The Imam discovered the truth and paid for it with his life. The ruler of Samarkand has called upon the aid of the cult of Tawil At'Umr, the First of the Ancient Ones and the Opener of the Way, the name on the forbidden sigil hidden in the sands of the Empty Quarter, where the faithful dare not tread. Vile sorcery and evil – evil older than time itself. The cult makes its lair in the ruins of an abandoned temple in the inner city; here is the sacrificial dagger steeped in blood and unhallowed prayers intoned from the unnameable book of the mad scholar Abdulqadir bin Hamad of Sanaa, who took the name al-Hazrat in blasphemous mockery of the Prophet. The Khan seeks to restore his rule through the powers of darkness, but he is mistaken; the High Priests of Tawil At'Umr heed no law other than that of the ones who inhabit the nameless gulfs beyond the celestial spheres."

"I know nothing of sorcery," said Nizam. "Yet with the Light of God at my side I fear no evil, of man or of *djinn*. If the Imam was right, we must stamp out this corruption, even at the cost of our lives."

"There are fates far worse than death, Emir. To behold the face of the Opener of the Way is to forfeit your soul; madness and damnation await all who gaze into the light of the luminous orbs that mark His arrival, into the black, formless essence in their midst."

"As will they be the reward of those who do nothing in the presence of evil." Nizam shook his head and turned to his men. "Perhaps the path that led us into this shining city does not lead out of it. I came to Samarkand to smite the enemies of the Sultan; it is my sworn duty before God. If any of you wish to leave, you are free to do so."

"The thing you speak of," said Amin, "may be deathless and eternal, but its followers are men, flesh and blood and fear. Night is our ally; there are many holes in the walls of the inner city."

Nizam stared into the eyes of the old scholar. "What say you, *alim*? Will you lead us into the temple, against the enemies of the Word?"

"Know that God is with those who ward against evil." The old man nodded and pulled the ends of his cloak closer together to hide the trembling of his gnarled hands.

***

THE PALE crescent moon rose in majestic silence, scattering silvery light across the towers and rooftops of the dreaming city. A sepulchral hush descended upon the age-old streets, broken only by the footsteps of the patrolling guards. The waning rays spilled over the crumbling walls of the *madinah*, where a black shape perched atop the ancient, dilapidated battlement. It slunk along the top of the wall until it stood above the *madinah* gate, where a lone sentry stood in the circle of yellow light cast by a torch.

A low rustle alerted the watchman; he began to turn, but a powerful blow below the left ear felled him senseless. Amin dragged the motionless form into the shadows and signalled into the darkness. Four silhouettes emerged from the dark side alley across the street and moved through the gate, melding with the darkness beyond. They navigated the deserted streets and secret passages of the inner city, halting in the shadows until the sound of approaching guards receded. Finally they reached a small square hidden between two larger buildings, where moonlight shone on the ruins of a square stone structure. Flat shapes of black basalt rock lay scattered in a rough circle around the temple. Dawud ran his fingers across the carved surface of one of the monoliths and drew his hand back as if from a flame.

"The symbol of Tawil At'Umr," he whispered, pointing at an etching of spheres joined by straight lines. A shudder passed through the Seljuks as they crossed the threshold of the temple. Nizam strained his eyes against the darkness: the temple was empty and smelled of must and age. Most of the roof had collapsed into a great pile of debris, but a cobwebbed alcove once occupied by the altar still stood in the far wall and the stumps of great pillars rose from the stone floor like the remains of broken teeth.

The moments trickled like hours, the men growing restless. Finally Haroun held up a silencing hand; footsteps approached from the dark street. A figure swathed in black entered the temple and picked its way across the rubble-strewn floor to the alcove. From the far wall came the creaking of levers and gears and the scraping of chains; a stone slab slid out of sight, revealing an open doorway. Before the noise died down, the Seljuk had reached the man standing in the doorway and cut his throat with a swift strike of his dagger. The cultist fell without a sound, his blood gushing black in the light of the moon.

The hidden entrance opened on a winding, descending staircase, lit by the flickering light of torches. A wave of indescribable stench, like a thousand open graves, welled from the depths of the passage and a distant, repeating chant reverberated from the walls. It was as if they stood in the very jaws of Hell.

"For the Sultan," whispered Nizam, stepping through the doorway. The men followed. With each turn of the stairs the air grew more stagnant, the stench more oppressive. The chanting increased in pitch, broken at times by wild cries and shrill, inhuman ululations. As he approached the bottom of the stairs, the nobleman halted and drew his sword, pointing to the shadows that flitted across the walls of the passage. Blades gleamed in the torch-light.

Before the guards at the steps could realize what was happening, the Seljuks sprang out of the passage. Nizam swung his sword in a wide horizontal arc and a head tumbled to the floor in a spray of blood, eyes wide with astonishment. Mahmoud hewed down two cultists as they reached for their knives and Haroun plunged his daggers into the throat of a fourth man, cutting off a shout of alarm. Covered in blood, the warriors cast their gaze around and their hearts sank from the sight.

The staircase had ended on a broad stone terrace overlooking a hall of immense proportions, lit by flames burning in great braziers. Its vaulted, charred ceiling rested on the shoulders of four colossal basalt statues shaped in the grotesque likeness of the blackest of nightmares. Beneath their feet stretched a sea of chanting, shrieking worshippers gathered around a circular pit in which darkness and mist bubbled and coalesced, hinting at the hideous form within. At the side of the pit stood an elevated platform with a black stone altar perched upon it. A dark-robed figure stood behind the shrine, its arms raised. Unearthly cries rose from its throat, to which the roiling mass in the pit responded with flashes of eerie light. As the luminous orbs appeared, a mad frenzy swept the revellers, the cacophony ascending to a delirious howl.

"The High Priest," Dawud said, pointing at the figure and the leathery shape laid across the altar. "Behold - the forbidden book!"

Black, tumorous tentacles emerged from the shimmering mist,

writhing and coiling across the stone floor. One of them wrapped itself around the naked, glistening body of a woman and she shrieked in a paroxysm of terror and ecstasy before vanishing into the boiling vapours of the pit.

"May the Light of God be with us." Nizam tilted his head to the steps leading down from the terrace. "Mahmoud and I will charge through the middle. Fight to the end - let no one escape." With that he raced down the steps and threw himself at the enemy, bellowing the name of the Almighty.

Terrified shrieks and death-screams rose from the unholy throng as the two Seljuks fell upon them with their swords drawn, hewing off limbs and heads. Most of the cultists were unarmed, and the ones with weapons were thrown into disarray. Using the distraction, Amin and Haroun skirted the melee and took shelter in the shadows between the burning braziers. The wanderer gazed at the black-robed figure upon the altar; the High Priest uttered a terrible curse and turned the pages of the book, his cries rising into the stale, noxious air.

"Kill the priest," he shouted to Haroun above the clamour of battle and leapt forward, dealing death with his sword. Mahmoud and Nizam had cleaved a red trail through the panicked crowd, but their foes outnumbered them ten to one; already the cultists were regrouping, forming a defensive wall before the altar. The black tentacles moved in rhythm with the blasphemous prayer, groping and flailing through the fleeing figures. Nizam hacked at a thick, slime-slick feeler, then brought the blade round to shield himself from the frenzied revellers. Mahmoud's great frame moved with the agility of a cat as he

traded blows with three defenders. Retreating before the lashing limbs of the horror from the pit that shivered with feeding frenzy, Amin felt the cold touch of the stone statue against his back. His gaze sought Haroun in the shadows around the altar and saw the lithe figure emerge behind the priest, daggers poised for the killing blow.

The calm, deep voice of the old scholar resonated from above with the words of the prayer of light. Before the astonished eyes of the cultists the tentacles began to shrivel and crumble to black dust; a terrible sound burst forth from the poisonous vapours of the pit. The warriors' spirits rallied. Nizam and Mahmoud cut through the ranks of their foes with renewed vigour, heedless of their wounds. The wanderer sprang atop the taloned foot of the basalt colossus, avoiding the slashes and stabs of the charging cultists; his fingers and toes seeking fissures in the stone, he began to climb up, toward the hideous, tentacled head. He paused in the nook of the arm of the idol to see a group of cultists rush the terrace through a hidden staircase and fall upon the praying Dawud with their knives. The old scholar cut down two attackers before a third ran him through, a cry of triumph on his lips.

From the bubbling chaos of the pit the tide of black slime surged once more, its thrashing limbs fastening upon the screaming bodies; a bulbous dark shape began to take form in their midst. The High Priest sensed danger and turned to face Haroun; the warrior stared into the lifeless depths of the black eyes and felt his resolve wane, the whisper of a vast, alien mind probe his thoughts. He raised his arm to strike and the dagger fell before his feet. A veil of darkness stole across his brain;

he thought and felt nothing as he descended the steps leading from the platform, as the blades of the worshippers hacked him to pieces.

Blood bubbled on Mahmoud's lips, but the giant still swung his heavy sword, bringing it down on a cultist's head like an axe. Out of the corner of his eye he saw a tentacle as thick as a man's torso loom above Nizam's head as the nobleman downed another opponent. With a roar that shook the temple the raven-haired warrior threw himself at the writhing monstrosity; the limb fastened itself around him, crushing his ribcage into his lungs and dragging him screaming into the seething mist. Nizam had little time to grieve, for the cultists closed on him in a flurry of blades. He slipped on the blood and slime and dropped to his knees; two men fell on him, knives seeking his throat. He kicked one aside, felt a hot, searing pain as the other knife missed his jugular vein by a whisper and sank deep into his shoulder.

Poised above the killing floor, the glassy eyes of the thing that hid in the skin of the High Priest followed the demise of the attackers, tittering as the giant Seljuk vanished into the black chaos of the pit. In an instant its telepathic senses flared in alarm; two powerful hands grasped its black robes and an irresistible force heaved it into the air, holding it above the tendrils of seething mist, above the luminous orbs that grew brighter in anticipation of the feeding. The body dropped with a bestial howl, the writhing, oozing mass gurgling around it as it sank.

The wanderer's fingers curled around the corners of the ancient tome on the altar. As he watched, the symbols on the pages seemed to squirm

and rearrange themselves; there was a flicker of strange sensation in his head, like a whistle of wind through the farthest reaches of his consciousness. He hesitated for a moment, then flung the book into the dark, putrescent depths.

The thing in the pit screamed; it was a scream that rippled through the mind, setting it ablaze with agony. Amin clasped his hands to his ears in a vain attempt to block the sound. A great rumble shook the foundations of the temple; cracks appeared in the vaulted ceiling and the stone horrors that bore its weight. The black mass vanished into the depths of the circular opening like a rat scurrying into the shadows. The wandered grasped his sword and leapt off the platform; shrieks filled the air as the panicked cultists crowded around the steps leading to the terrace and the way out of the collapsing temple.

Trapped beneath the snarling cultist, Nizam summoned the last vestiges of his strength and drove his knee into the attacker's groin. As the man yelped in pain, the nobleman grabbed his knife-hand by the elbow and wrist and twisted; the blade turned, the weight of the cultist driving it into his neck. The Seljuk shoved the dead body away and rose to his feet as the tremor almost knocked him back down. Strong arms seized him by the shoulders; it was the wanderer, pointing to an arched doorway in the base of one of the statues.

They raced up the hidden staircase and emerged at the foot of the passage leading above just as one of the great statues crumbled, bringing an entire section of the ceiling down on the heads of the screaming worshippers. A melee had broken out

22

on the stairs leading to the terrace, those above trampling those underfoot in a surge of animal terror. Amin and Nizam raced up the steps, stopping only once they emerged from the ruins of the temple and into the square around it, the starry sky above their heads. Before their unbelieving eyes, the dilapidated walls of the ruin began to fold into themselves, the entire structure tumbling into some hidden dimension, an invisible pocket of space. In the wake of its fall there was a hint of strange forms and angles, of the darkness that reigns in the lightless realms beyond space and time; Amin averted his gaze from the swirling chaos of the vortex, but Nizam's eyes filled with the unthinkable sight, his mind surrendering to the blackness of the void.

Terrified and covered in blood, the wanderer stood in the middle of an empty square, the dead body of his commander at his feet, its visage twisted in a hideous mask of terror that would haunt him until the end of his days. The walls of the temple had vanished and the monoliths gave off a low, sinister light. He turned and fled, and did not stop until dawn crested the mountains and the towers and minarets of Samarkand lay in the distance; for now he knew its elegant splendour to be a mirage, an illusion beneath which black horrors slept, dreaming of flight from the abyss they inhabited, of once again ruling the world of men.

ABOUT THE AUTHOR

DAMIR SALKOVIC is an aficionado of weird and macabre tales, born and raised in Sarajevo, Bosnia-Herzegovina, presently residing in Virginia, USA. He is an obsessive reader of horror, fantasy and sci-fi stories, preferably from the pulp magazine era. His stories have been published on the *Tales of the Zombie Wars* fan-fiction website and as part of the *Tales to Terrify* podcast. He earns his living as an accountant, a profession that lends itself well to nightmares and harrowing visions.

THE HOUSE OF SKULLS
Gavin Chappell

1 The Silent Raiders

THE PALL of smoke that had loomed over the savannah since dawn came from the village on the horizon. As Yeduza directed her scouts forward, she felt a cold claw of anticipation clutch at her heart. Had they finally found the trail of the raiders?

The scouts loped silently forward, casting cautious glances to left and right as they approached the palisade that surrounded the collection of blackened, thatched huts. Soon they were out of sight from the main army.

Yeduza sat her horse patiently. The warriors of the Nago waited in silence, ostrich-plume headdresses nodding on their heads, their assegais a fence of steel as the hot sun beat down from a sky like burnished brass. Around them, the dusty savannah stretched towards an endless horizon, red earth and yellow grasses broken only by thickets of thorn bushes and occasional baobab trees that thrust dry branches towards the steely skies. Throughout the disciplined ranks of spearmen and horsemen, there was not a sound.

Yeduza looked up as the scouts returned from the burning village, running across the withered grass towards her position. Their leader had the aquiline nose and straight hair of a

Bengue herder from the north. His dark face was pale, his eyes wide and glassy. Yeduza knew he was a man who had seen many wars since Emperor Mtogo seized the throne of Nago. Whatever he had seen in the guttered village must be truly horrific.

He pointed back the way he had come, and shook his head. 'They've been here,' he said thickly. 'They've been here only recently.'

'Any survivors?' Yeduza snapped.

The Bengue scout shook his head, his eyes troubled. 'All dead, or taken,' he muttered.

Yeduza looked back at her warriors. Troop after troop, they stood or sat motionless in the hot sun, awaiting her orders. She kicked her horse forward.

'I will see this,' she said. 'Some of you, come with me.'

Twelve warriors rode forward, each one a tough, hard-bitten Amazon of Mtogo's personal guard like Yeduza herself. Like her, each wore her hair elaborately coiffured with loam to resembled bull's horns, and identical scars criss-crossed their cheeks. Each bore an assegai in her right hand, a hippopotamus-hide shield in her left.

She nodded to the Bengue scout, and he trotted alongside her as they rode cautiously into the centre of the village.

Huts smoked or blazed on either side. Cooking pots, broken calabashes, and dead chickens littered the hard-packed red earth. Yeduza encountered no sign of habitation until she saw an old man sitting in the shade of a tree. As she guided her unwilling horse closer, she saw the man's body had been hacked in two like a pig in the marketplace. Red,

writhing worms of guts pooled beside him, in the shadow of the tree.

The riders turned a corner and found themselves in the central space of the village. Where the villagers had once held their market, now was a scene of slaughter.

Severed heads leered from stakes, watching with glassy eyes as the Nago warriors approached. Black blood pooled on the earth.

A flock of vultures leapt into the air as the warriors entered the open space, and circled above, screeching and cackling. The butchered corpses they had abandoned were almost stripped of flesh. A cooking pot hung from an iron stand above still smoking embers.

Yeduza could see too few bodies for this heap of corpses to represent the entire population of the village. Gagging at the stench of death, she dismounted to speak to the scout.

'Where are the rest?' she demanded. 'What have they done to the others? These are only old people, or small children. What happened to the youths of the village?'

The Bengue shrugged. 'Perhaps the raiders took them to sell as slaves,' he replied.

'No,' said one of the Amazons. Yeduza turned to look at the woman, a tall, ill-favoured female called Ngiri. 'The raiders take no slaves. They spare only those who will join them – become like them.'

Yeduza gave Ngiri an appraising look. She strode across to the cooking pot and inserted a finger to test the heat of its contents. The mess of millet and vegetables was still warm.

'They cannot be far away,' she said, a note of urgency in her voice.

Her companions numbered only fourteen, and the raiders must still be nearby. A chill of fear ran down her spine. The contents of the cooking pot, disturbed by her questing finger, bubbled. Something bobbed up to the top. Yeduza felt cold sweat break out on her skin.

Floating on the surface was a small human hand.

A roar of many voices alerted Yeduza, and she whirled round. The noise came from outside the village, where she had left her forces.

'They're under attack!' Ngiri exclaimed. 'The raiders?'

'Who else?' Yeduza seized the pommel of her horse's saddle and swung herself up. She cursed herself for being drawn off into the village while the cannibal raiders had massed elsewhere, leaving her troops leaderless while she satisfied morbid curiosity. She brandished her assegai towards the sound of battle. 'Follow me!' she cried, and spurred her horse into a gallop.

The Bengue scout sprinted to keep up as the other riders cantered after her.

They rode out from the huts to see the troops of Nago on the plain before them under attack from hundreds of ghastly figures, men in the brief garb of villagers, faces and limbs daubed a chalk-white. Armed with assegais and sickle-bladed swords, the raiders came on in an awful silence. Yeduza's warriors recoiled before their eerie onslaught.

Desperate, Yeduza galloped her horse towards the centre of the crumbling line. She shrieked the 'Yeee!' battle cry of the Nagos, plunged her assegai into the white-painted breast of a silent attacker. Her charge dragged the speared body past and behind her through the dust, but still the man clutched at the blade. Yeduza twisted her arm and hauled the assegai out of his guts. To her horror, she saw him rise once more to his feet.

The impetus of her charge had carried her into the raiders' ranks. Her horse whinnied and rose on its hind-legs as white-painted faces leered all around her. The raider she had speared shuffled after them, dragging a sword alongside it.

Then horses were on either side of Yeduza, riding into the crowd, the Amazons on their backs thrusting assegais into raiders who rose again and again to tear at their assailants with clawed hands. Grimacing, Yeduza thrust her assegai directly into the painted face of another raider. Her blade jutted from the back of the man's skull and he fell back to twitch among the thundering hoofs of the attacking Nago horses. She did not see whether he died.

Yeduza swivelled in her saddle and called to her troops, cavalry and infantry.

'Fight! Fight, children of Nago! Fight and die, for our Emperor Mtogo! Fight for Nago!'

The Nagos rushed forward, cutting and hacking at the silent raiders; many fell to their deadly foes, but others struggled on. Yeduza urged them on as she led her riders deeper into the fray. The dust hung in thick clouds around the battlefield, almost blotting out the blazing sun. As Yeduza fought on, a booming, belling note rang out across the embattled armies.

At once, the silent raiders drew back, their voiceless multitude dividing to open up an avenue. The Nago warriors halted and looked to Yeduza for orders. Yeduza's attention was on the gap in the crowd, and the figure that rode towards her down the avenue of warriors. So, this was the leader of the raiders who had swarmed up from the southern jungles, locust-like, to ransack Mtogo's empire!

She saw a tall man, easily seven foot high, his skin the jet-black of the jungle tribes. Long, curling locks of hair hung down his broad back. Round his throat, he wore a choker of bones, and a kilt of snakeskins hung from his waist. He bore an assegai in one hand, a hippopotamus-hide shield like Yeduza's own in the other. The glossy skin of his face was daubed a ghastly white. But it was his eyes that caught and seized Yeduza's gaze.

They were cold and merciless. Snake eyes, Yeduza found herself thinking as the man rode closer. The eyes of a python, mesmerising its prey.

Silence hung heavy over the battlefield as the horseman trotted closer to Yeduza.

He cast a questing, probing glance at the ranks of Nago footmen and cavalry, then spoke in a rolling, booming voice

'Who is the leader of this rabble?' he called. 'Has the coward Mtogo come to fight his foe, the Kikwenzi?'

So that was what they called themselves. Yet it was these white-painted Kikwenzi who were the rabble, not the armies of Mtogo. She stirred in

her saddle and the tall man turned his glittering serpent gaze upon her.

'You?' he boomed, incredulously. 'Do you lead these warriors? Does Mtogo send a woman to face me? I'll give you to my minions, make you their plaything!'

'I am Yeduza, captain of Mtogo's bodyguard, general of his armies,' Yeduza replied angrily. 'I have fought for him since his youth, when he took the land of Nago from Mungu-Ovu who ruled as a tyrant from the House of Skulls! I shall strike you down, you and your bandit army! Who are you to challenge the Emperor?'

'I am Chinja,' the tall man replied. 'I am Warlord of the Kikwenzi.' He indicated the silent ranks on his either hand. Their blank eyes gazed upon the scene as blindly as the eye sockets of skulls in some mausoleum. Yeduza felt a chill run down her spine, but she shook off her fear and brandished her assegai.

'Let us fight it out, you and I,' she proposed, as Chinja's snakelike gaze held her. 'Why should our people die? Let us fight in single combat, before our armies, and let the loser leave this land.' Her voice rang with a confidence that was not entirely unfounded. Few had defeated her in the many years that she had fought for her Emperor.

She remembered how she had struggled to defeat those Kikwenzi she had fought, and shivered.

Chinja laughed. He leapt down from his horse and advanced, carrying assegai and shield. 'Very well then!' he boomed, and his assegai blade flashed in the bright sunlight. 'Come fight me.'

Yeduza leapt down from her own horse, flung its reins into the hands of the nearest warrior, and stamped across the red earth to meet her challenger.

They faced each other, the Nago Amazon, her scarred face emotionless, her assegai held steady; the tall raider chieftain, his eyes cold and glittering. They began to circle, as the massed ranks looked on, each probing forward with their assegai, each bearing their shield before them to meet the other's attack.

Yeduza's naked feet padded on the hard earth; her assegai flashed in the sunlight; Chinja's shield met it, turned its blow, and then his own assegai shot forward, aiming under Yeduza's lifted shield. She leapt back, then thrust her assegai at Chinja's unprotected shoulder. Chinja parried the thrust with his own assegai and the crack of wood meeting wood rang out across the savannah.

Yeduza charged forward, shield in front of her, and smashed into Chinja's own shield, sending him staggering back. He jabbed awkwardly at her with his assegai, and its razor-sharp edge sliced through the ostrich plumes that nodded on her head.

Yeduza lunged, feinted, and waited until the man brought his shield up, then lunged again, going in under its lower edge, sinking in. Yeduza put all her weight and strength behind that blow. She saw the assegai vanish under the shield until over half its length was gone, yet she felt nothing. She stared at her opponent in bewilderment.

Those snake-eyes seized her again. She pulled back her assegai. What witchcraft was this? No blood was visible on its tip. Chinja drew his shield aside, and she saw that his torso was unmarked. And yet she had thrust the assegai in for half its length...

Chinja laughed at her incredulity, then lunged with his assegai. Despite her horror and confusion, Yeduza succeeded in lifting her heavy shield to counter the blow, but this was what Chinja had been waiting for. Copying her own trick, he thrust his assegai under her shield rim. She felt it sink deep into her thigh, tearing and ripping through skin and flesh and sinking deep into bone. In the last moment before consciousness departed, Yeduza knew that if she survived this wound, it would cripple her.

As she fell heavily to the red earth, she heard, as if from the end of a long subterranean tunnel, the pounding of feet as the Kikwenzi charged the Nago ranks.

2   Treachery

DOWN A long, booming well of darkness, Yeduza heard someone calling her name. She struggled up through black, viscous tar that clung to her, threatening to drag her back down into the roaring deeps.

Her eyes cracked open, and sunlight stabbed into her mind. Her mouth was as dry as a desert. She felt a throbbing pain from her leg. Looming over her was Ngiri.

Yeduza rose on her elbow. She caught a glimpse of hunched figures surrounding her before it all began to spin and she slumped back.

'Lie back, Yeduza,' Ngiri said quietly. 'You are weak. Do nothing, and all will be well.'

Yeduza looked up at her. 'The Kikwenzi? Chinja?'

Ngiri snorted scornfully. 'They sent us into retreat.' She studied the blood-crusted bandages that adorned her sleek limbs. 'After you fell, they charged us. It was a difficult matter to drag you away.'

'Chinja?' Yeduza asked again. 'Did you kill him?' She looked down at her thigh, to see it wrapped with healing pergularia leaves. When Ngiri said nothing, she looked up again, trying to quell the waves of nausea that rushed through her body.

Ngiri shook her head curtly. 'All who faced him were slain. You were lucky. He only crippled you.' She indicated Yeduza's leg. 'The bone is shattered.'

Yeduza shook her head. 'Help me up,' she said thickly. 'Help me up now, damn you! Where is my horse?'

A little unwillingly, Ngiri helped her general to her feet. Yeduza looked around the camp. They must have ridden far from the battlefield before halting here. She was shocked to see the army had been thinned by at least half. It was close to evening.

'My horse!' Yeduza snapped. Ngiri led the animal forward, and Yeduza struggled painfully to climb into the saddle. Ngiri stood by, looking on in silence.

'You should rest,' she said distantly. 'You will not heal without rest. You will be weak for some time.'

Yeduza glared down at her. 'Don't speak about weakness,' she hissed painfully. 'I must address my troops. We go after Chinja.'

Ngiri shook her head. 'Do you not understand?' she taunted Yeduza. 'The raiders defeated you. You were lucky to survive. Tomorrow, we must return to Mnara, where Mtogo will hear all that has happened, and pass judgement.'

Yeduza stared coldly down at Ngiri. Did the woman seek to supplant her? Did she think that this defeat, this wound, would finish her? She was captain of Mtogo's bodyguard, general of the armies of Nago! She…

A wave of giddiness washed over her, and she slumped over the horse's neck.

She needed rest.

***

THE NEXT morning, the defeated, diminished army of Nago hurried back across the burnt and looted land that the Kikwenzi had raided. The news of the defeat spread across the grasslands like wildfire, and those villages through which they had ridden were deserted. Yeduza assumed the villagers had fled into the bush.

She rode in silence at the head of the command group, her face showing the bleakness of the vanquished. She had failed, and now she was crippled. Perhaps Mtogo's physicians would be able to set her shattered bone so it grew straight again, but it seemed doubtful. As a cavalry-woman, she was not as badly affected by the wound as would a foot soldier be, yet it meant more than that. It reminded her of her failure to defeat Chinja, of the knowledge that the battle had been lost.

It was a sign of weakness, and she knew that Ngiri, who rode close behind her wearing a jackal's grin, saw it as an indication that Yeduza's glory days were over; that the day had come when Ngiri would rise into the ascendant. And what would that mean for Yeduza?

On the third day, they crested a rise and saw the Nago River snaking away across the savannah. Directly before them, built in a looping curve of the river, stood the walled city of Mnara, capital of Mtogo's empire. They rode towards the great eastern gates, built of ebony from the southern jungles, standing in the thick adobe wall like the portal of some titan. The guards at the gates had flung them open at the approach of the great army, and already the streets beyond were lined with grim-faced townsfolk as Yeduza trotted in at the head of the column. Horsemen rode behind her, and behind them the spearmen marched, their weapons at slant. The street wound up through the solid, foursquare, flat-roofed buildings - houses, shops, and temples of smooth, sculpted adobe - towards the great palace of Mtogo. Yeduza remembered that day, many years ago, when at the end of a long siege Mnara had opened its gates to Mtogo and his rebels; when she had ridden at Mtogo's side as he went to his final encounter with Mungu-Ovu, in the House of Skulls that had stood where now the palace reared its adobe walls. He had slain that tyrant in his house of the dead, and all had hailed him as a hero.

It was with sadness that Yeduza looked upon her lord, the Emperor, where he lolled on his golden throne beneath an awning of lion-skin, surrounded by the officials of his court and the ladies of his harem. Age and the cares of state had dulled the eyes that once shone with ardour to bring down a tyrant. His body, once supple and lithe, was running to seed, and a paunch oozed over his leopard-skin loincloth. He thrust his hand into a brass bowl of mealies and stuffed them into his mouth, barely acknowledging his returning general.

'Hail, king of kings,' Yeduza said, after climbing painfully down from her horse and going to kneel before him. 'I return with news of defeat. The Kikwenzi crushed us, sent us into flight. We need reinforcements if we are to defeat them.'

Silence reigned. Mtogo cocked his gold-crowned head. His eyes fell upon Yeduza's leaf-bandaged leg. 'You are weak,' he remarked.

That word again! Yeduza drew herself up painfully, and returned the emperor's gaze. 'I was wounded in my fight with Chinja, chief of the Kikwenzi. No doubt your physicians will set it right, and I will be able to take to the field again.'

Mtogo snorted. 'No doubt,' he said contemptuously. Yeduza was hurt by his unwelcoming attitude. This was not the reception of an old and trusted retainer. The king of kings stirred his corpulent rump.

'And word comes to me that this defeat came whilst you slept,' Mtogo added, thrusting his hand into the bowl of mealies. He ate greedily while watching her face.

Yeduza's skin went cold, as if a cloud had drifted across the blazing sun. Her mouth dry, she said, 'Never, my lord, I...'

'I sent you to fight the raiders. You slept when you should be fighting.' He shook his head sadly then grinned. 'You are no longer my general.'

Yeduza stared at him in anger. This was unjust! She had fought; she had been wounded in his service… Who had told him these lies? Word had come to him… She looked suspiciously up at Ngiri and saw to her shock that the woman was hefting her assegai.

She looked back at Mtogo. The man's eyes glittered. He nodded.

'Kill her,' he hissed. Ngiri raised her assegai.

3   The Forest

AS THE wickedly sharp tip of Ngiri's weapon hissed towards her, she flung herself to one side, hitting the hard packed earth with a gasp as her wounded leg sent a stab of pain throughout her body. She caught a glimpse of the Nago warriors staring down at the scene in consternation; of Mtogo rising from his throne, bellowing orders. Ngiri lifted her assegai again. Yeduza had left her own weapon with her horse. She rolled towards her, grabbing her bare feet and toppling her before the Amazon could spit her. Ngiri went crashing down at Mtogo's feet. Yeduza forced herself up, grabbing Ngiri's assegai as she did so.

'Make your obeisances well,' Yeduza said, as Ngiri seemed to grovel at Mtogo's feet. 'But I shall not remain to bow my neck before a tyrant.'

As Mtogo's cold eyes turned to her, regarding her like a python staring at a rodent, Yeduza leapt astride her horse.

'Take her down!' Mtogo bellowed. 'A hundredweight of gold to whoever brings me her head! She conspires to seize my throne!'

As the confused warriors ran to surround their erstwhile general, Yeduza looked down at Mtogo in silence. Then she spurred her horse, and rode straight at the unwilling warriors. They scattered. Riders came to intercept the escapee. Yeduza downed one with a thrust of her assegai, took another's attack in her hastily raised hippopotamus-hide shield, and galloped across a clear space towards the city streets.

'Bring her back to me!' Mtogo shouted. 'Bring me her head!' But by now, Yeduza was charging through the southern gate of the city.

He turned coldly to look down at Ngiri, still prone before him, and he sat down upon his throne.

'Rise, Ngiri,' he said irritably. 'Take your best riders, and pursue Yeduza. If you bring me her head, you will replace her. If not, your own head will be the foundation stone of my House of Skulls.'

Ngiri rose, looked shakingly at her lord, and went to gather her best riders from among the confusion in the courtyard.

***

A WEEK later, Ngiri and her riders returned, empty-handed and many of them on foot.

'We pursued her south to the edge of the jungle,' Ngiri told Mtogo. 'But she didn't stop there; she simply rode on into the trees. We pursued as far as we could, but our horses began to die, and many of us became feverish.'

'Those jungles are a sinkhole of pestilence and corruption,' Mtogo murmured. 'Horses die; people die. Yeduza will not survive there. The wound in her leg will rot; she will die in agony, in the silence of the forest. We need not concern ourselves with her ambitions…'

Ngiri knelt proudly before the Emperor. 'Then I have fulfilled your commands,' she boasted. 'I become captain of your bodyguard, general of the armies of Nago!'

Mtogo gazed far off, as if into undreamt of vistas. Suddenly he shook his head, and turned his cold gaze upon Ngiri.

'What's this?' he rumbled. 'You lie! I ordered you to bring me her head. You failed.' Mtogo nodded to one of his companions, a muscular man, naked but for a loincloth. He drew a broad, sickle-blade sword and stepped forward.

Ngiri's face fell and shortly after, her head followed. It lay in the dust, ringed by a sticky pool of gore, until Mtogo lifted it up by the spiked locks, and laughed.

***

THE HORSE died after the second day in the jungle. As she limped away from its unmoving form, using her assegai as a crutch, Yeduza feared that she would soon join it. Her wound was a festering agony, and her sweat-slick body quivered involuntarily as she staggered on into the depths. In the dank, oppressive gloom of the forest, she felt confused, weak, lost. The trees grew higher and higher on either side, lianas hung down like stranglers' garrottes,

and she had no idea where she was going, and little notion where she had come from. The cries of birds and beasts echoed from the canopy above, or filtered through the dark wall of green that surrounded her. Her bare feet splashed through thick mud, and sometimes she saw snakes slithering away into the gloom. It was a dark, awful place.

She had ridden far and fast; the horse had almost died under her even during the flight across the savannah. Her pursuers had seemed relentless until she plunged into the trackless, waving depths of the jungle. Then the pursuit had faltered, died after a day or two. Much like her horse.

Why had Mtogo wanted her killed? The question had rattled around inside her skull throughout the long escape. They had fought side by side in the old days, and he had favoured her throughout his reign. Now it seemed he would cast her aside like a broken calabash. Had Ngiri poisoned his ear against her? Had the woman even now taken her place? Yeduza had been one of the highest in the land; now, after a single encounter with Chinja, all that had changed. Her lord reviled her, her subordinates plotted against her; she had been pursued from the land like a defeated lion chased from the pride. Now, here she was in the depths of the jungle from which came little more than pestilence, disease, rumours of war… It was said that a mighty kingdom lay further to the south; an empire hacked from the forest. Traders had spoken of its expansion in recent years. But that was still far, far to the south. Endless leagues of desolate jungle stretched away before her, deserted except for deadly animals and lethal disease.

Sweat was pouring down her face. As she looked about her, the forest seemed to wheel, its sinister gloom a blur of darkness. Yeduza heard a pounding in her brain. She reached up an arm to dash the sweat from her eyes. Her sight was growing dim. She fell forward helplessly, unaware that she was falling until she sank into the thick clay of the forest floor. The last thing she saw confirmed her suspicions that the sickness was taking control of her brain, as she seemed to see tiny men stepping from the trees to squat at her side, staring down at her in amazement. Then all was darkness.

***

YEDUZA AWOKE, feeling strangely refreshed. Soft daubs of light dappled the forest floor. Her nausea and fever had left her, the pain had gone from her leg, and she felt strong and invigorated. She was lying on a bed of leaves.

She lifted herself on one elbow to inspect her leg, and halted in amazement, wondering if the fever dream still remained. Three small men crouched at the side of the clearing, watching her. She stared at them, and they returned her gaze unafraid. Then one of them spoke, a venerable, grizzled old fellow, naked like the rest except for a loincloth.

'Your sickness has gone. We mended your leg as best we could' - Yeduza looked down at it, and saw that the swelling and discolouration had gone, but it looked crooked, twisted —'but you will be lame for the rest of your life.'

Yeduza rose slowly, cautiously, and tested the leg. It pained her, with a dull, nagging ache, but she could stand on it. She looked down at the three little men,

wonderingly. They seemed real, no figment of her fevered mind.

'Who are you?' she asked slowly.

The older man smiled. 'Our own name we keep to ourselves,' he said in a deep rumbling voice. 'But your folk call us the Mbilikimo.'

Yeduza's eyes widened. She had been told stories of the Mbilikimo, the pygmies of the forest, when she was a child. They were said to be fierce hunters, despite their small size, expert trackers who could vanish at will. But she had thought them nothing more than fireside tales.

'Then I have you to thank for my life,' she said, half questioningly. The elder pygmy nodded.

'It was Dogo who found you,' he said, and indicated a handsome young pygmy on his right, who carried a bow over his sinewy shoulders. 'He hunts far and wide, alone in the forest. He returned from one of his forays with a tale of a great warrior-woman lying near death in the swamp; urged us to come to her aid. He would not listen to our deliberations but took several hunters and brought you back. Our best healers tended you, and did what they could.'

Dogo nodded. 'I hoped you would aid us against Chatu,' he said, in a low voice.

Yeduza sat down slowly. It seemed her healing came at a price. But who was Chatu? Another pygmy?

'Chatu is a python,' said the pygmy elder when she asked. 'He is a tyrant who oppresses us, and demands our children as sacrifices, or takes them himself.'

'A python?' Yeduza asked. 'A snake?'

The elder shook his head. 'More than a snake,' he rumbled. 'Chatu is a demon. He was set to lord it over us when the evil ones marched through our lands. They fled up from the south, where they had seen much fighting. There is a kingdom of people like you far south of here, and it was from there that our oppressors came. They took our youths and maidens and enslaved them. Young Dogo was forced to cut wood and carry burdens for them. Our maidens were ravished. Others of our people they ate as if they were mere beasts. The oppression was woeful.

'I spoke to the elders of the other clans, and we went before their leader, a snake-eyed sorcerer, to beg him to end this oppression. He told us that his people were moving north, but that they would set one of their gods to watch over us. Now we must make offerings to this god, Chatu. He is a huge serpent who dwells among the rocks near our camp, and it is there that we must leave our sacrifices.'

Dogo added; 'They took me and the other slaves along on their march north. They devoured many of us. I escaped with barely my life and returned to find that all was as it is now. We are powerless against the python, but I know that your people are strong, and mighty warriors. You can prevail where our people would be slain.'

Yeduza studied them abstractedly. 'A snake-eyed sorcerer?' she asked. 'Did his warriors daub themselves with white?'

Dogo nodded. 'They follow him under a spell.'

'Chinja!' Yeduza said, with a curse. 'I know him. He gave me this wound. And he set this python to oppress you?'

'You know of the sorcerer?' the elder asked. Yeduza nodded.

'He attacked my people too,' she said. 'They killed many people in their raids. Where they are now, I do not know.' She rose. 'It seems we have a common enemy. Well, I owe you a debt for healing my leg. I shall fight against your python, though whether I will succeed now that I am a cripple, I cannot say.'

***

THE ROCKS beyond the pygmies' camp were a wilderness of boulders in a great barren clearing near a swamp. Yeduza stood at their edge, with her assegai in one hand and her shield in the other. Dogo, who had led her there, stood at her side, watching her silently.

Her heart was heavy with doubt. Could she prevail over a demonic python? It seemed that she must try, for the sake of these tiny people who had taken her in and healed her when she was wounded and alone. She looked down at Dogo.

'Chatu dwells among those rocks,' the pygmy told her.

She nodded. 'I shall find him.' She left his side and advanced, picking her way across the loose shale and squeezing between boulders, looking back from time to time. Soon the pygmy had been swallowed up by the darkness of the trees.

Yeduza saw no signs of life, but as she advanced through the barren area, she caught a whiff of a strange, musky scent. The rocks seemed to tower over her as she moved through them, assegai poised and ready.

She whirled round at a noise from behind her, heart thudding in her chest. The rocks she had traversed were bare and empty. The forest was a distant wall of gloom. She studied the rocks for some time, but saw nothing. Then she turned and walked on.

Again, a slither from her right. She turned, assegai poised. Nothing. She began to back away, her eyes vigilant as she searched the rocks. The slither came again, from behind her, and she spun on the balls of her feet, her assegai thrust out in front of her. She caught a glimpse of a dark, scaled form slithering away into the cover of the rocks.

The wind moaned among the boulders. Dust swirled in the sunlight. Yeduza paced across the sand towards the rocks where she had seen something move. If her glimpse was anything to go on, Chatu must be huge...Her heart pounded in her chest. Could she hope to defeat such an unnatural being?

She scrambled to the top of the rocks and looked down. To her mixed disappointment and relief, she saw nothing. As she stood looking down, she heard a scrape from the direction which she had come from. She turned, overbalanced and half jumped, half fell to the sand. As she did, she caught a glimpse of a dark, scaled tail slithering into cover.

Leaning on her assegai, she limped forwards. A short defile led into another sandy stretch. It was empty.

Yeduza turned to go back, and halted. Her blood froze despite the baking heat of the sun. Winding rapidly down the rocks ahead of her was the scaly length of the largest snake Yeduza had ever seen.

It reared up at her, jaws gaping.

Yeduza brought up her shield, and deflected Chatu's blunt head. It swayed back and forth, and flung itself at her again, trying to envelop her in its coils. She realised the snake had been accustomed to regular offerings, pygmy children who put up no resistance, not a Nago Amazon. She stabbed at Chatu with her assegai but it swarmed up the shaft. She dropped the assegai with a clatter.

The snake slithered forward. As Yeduza turned to run, her lame leg crumpled beneath her and she toppled to the rocky ground. Then the snake was on her, wrapping its smooth, scaly coils around her body. She struggled desperately, but now the snake was encircling her upper arms, pinioning them with incredible strength.

Now it looped round her neck, tightening until stars exploded in the growing darkness of her mind. Dimly, she saw its gaping jaws open above her head, widening to an incredible extent, wide enough to swallow her.... The snake was about to swallow her and she could do nothing. Its tongue flickered in and out, then its jaws sank down to envelop Yeduza's head.

It started back suddenly, lashing about in pain, releasing its grip on Yeduza. Blood spewed from its fanged mouth. Its long black tongue protruded from Yeduza's own mouth. The Amazon had bitten off its tongue.

The snake writhed and twisted, flinging Yeduza to one side. She spat the tongue out and scrabbled at the rocky ground until her hand closed on the worn shaft of her assegai. Desperately, clumsily, she brought it up alongside her face and rammed it into the writhing serpent. The creature's spasms tore the assegai from her hand. A chance flick of its huge tail sent Yeduza flying across the rocks. She lay there, dazed, listening to the creature's dying spasms. When at last it was still, Yeduza got unsteadily to her feet. She went to look at where the serpent lay, and halted.

Lying among the rocks, where the snake had been, was an immensely tall, thin man with blood dribbling from his tongueless mouth. The assegai projected from his chest. As Yeduza dragged it free, she saw the familiar white paint that daubed his bloody face. She leant on her assegai and pondered.

Thoughts of vengeance were on her mind.

4   A Ravaged Land

YEDUZA STOOD in the midst of the pygmy camp. Her friends sat beneath the towering trunks and gazed worshipfully up at her. Dogo regarded her with an appraising look. The elder, whose name was Mkongwe, looked on as a group of pygmy girls came shyly forward to place a garland of blossoms around their saviours' neck.

'This is a great honour,' Yeduza said, and she meant it, though the pygmies' adulation was a meagre thing beside that she had once known from the Nago. 'But Chatu's death will not make the lands safe from the Kikwenzi. I fought Chinja, their chief, and could not kill him. Even now, his silent raiders may be ravaging the Nago Empire. I want to stop him. Maybe if I did, my lord the Emperor would accept me as his general again.'

'Then you will not stay with us?' Dogo asked, suddenly. 'I… We hoped you would remain. As an honoured guest.'

Yeduza smiled at the little man. 'I thank you,' she said with good grace. 'But I cannot remain here while my people suffer. If there was only some way I could defeat Chinja…'

'You could not kill him last time,' Dogo said. 'What hope will you have now?'

Yeduza looked down at the leaf litter at her feet. 'But I must try,' she muttered fiercely.

Mkongwe spoke. 'We are indebted to you,' he said. 'And though he does not say, Dogo has knowledge that is vital to your ambition. You freed us from the scourge of Chatu. Now Dogo must tell you what you need to know – how Chinja may be killed.'

Yeduza looked at the young pygmy angrily. 'You know this?' she demanded. 'How? And why did you not say earlier?'

Dogo looked briefly ashamed. 'I had hoped you would stay,' he said. 'Very well, I will tell you what I discovered when I was a slave of the Kikwenzi.

'Before they attacked your lands, they skirted them to the north to find easier pickings, and to amass a larger army. They fall upon unsuspecting villages and slaughter all but the young and fit. The girls become camp followers; the youths become bearers or warriors. The warriors are ensorcelled by Chinja. They become zombies, in his thrall, killing and looting at his command, with no will of their own. That is why they are silent.

'North of your country they reached a great wasteland of sand, where little grew and few dwelt. Those who did live there were pale skinned folk who wrapped themselves in white robes. They rode on creatures like your own steed, or stranger beasts, and attacked with weapons that killed from afar with a great thunderclap. Against these warriors the Kikwenzi could not prevail, and even Chinja, whose magic makes him invulnerable to spears or swords, was wounded in the battle. As soon as he had been struck, he ordered a retreat and the mighty Kikwenzi horde fled in confusion. It was during that rout that I seized my chance to escape, and return here.'

Yeduza listened to his account, electrified.

'When was this?' she demanded.

'The moon has waxed and waned only nine times since I fled the Kikwenzi,' Dogo replied.

'Nine moons,' Yeduza murmured to herself. 'Then it was only shortly afterwards that they began their assault on Nago... The deserts of the North? Yes, I had heard that the Tiburi nomads raid the caravans with these *muskets*, as they are called. We have never ridden against them in my lifetime. But perhaps now is the time to forge links between their folk and ours.'

She took up her assegai and shield from where she had propped them against a tree. 'I thank you, Mbilikimo, for all you have done for me. I think I have fulfilled my obligations to you also. Now I must travel north, and find if I cannot trade with the Tiburi, gain one of these muskets – and use it against Chinja. Farewell.'

She turned to leave the clearing in haste. Dogo looked at Mkongwe then bounded after her.

'But you will not go alone?' he asked. 'Let me guide you through the jungle at least.' He looked hesitantly at Mkongwe again. 'That is, if the elder allows it.'

Mkongwe nodded. 'Let Dogo guide you,' he begged Yeduza. She looked down at the young pygmy.

'Very well,' she said impatiently. 'But we must make haste. The empire is at stake.'

A broad grin bloomed on Dogo's face.

***

SEVERAL DAYS later, they came out of the jungle. Beyond them, the flat, wide, sun-scorched expanse of the savannah stretched to a distant and dusty horizon.

'We are now in your lands,' the pygmy said, leaning on the blowpipe he had brought with him for hunting - and for defence. 'What do you wish to do?'

Yeduza turned to look down at her smaller companion with an expression of respect. He had proved an expert guide as they had journeyed under the dark, lowering eaves of the trees, leading her away from the many dangers that lurked in the depths of the jungle, helping her cross crocodile-infested rivers and navigate bottomless swamps. A bond had been created by their shared hardships.

'I must travel on to the northern deserts,' she told him. 'This is where we must say farewell.'

38

Dogo stared in the direction of the forest wall, disconsolate. 'Perhaps,' he said after a while, 'perhaps I... '

But Yeduza was ignoring him, scanning the horizon with her keen eyes. She pointed.

'Look!' she said. She was indicating a smoke trail that reached up into the cobalt blue skies. Dogo turned to look. His eyes flickered back and forth.

'And over there,' he said. Yeduza saw he was pointing at two more thick black smoke trails to the west. She cursed, knowing what this meant.

'Chinja has returned,' she muttered.

They reached the closest village towards evening, and discovered a scene that was grimly familiar to Yeduza. Bodies lay strewn about the mud streets, huts were guttering shells. Near the middle of the village, they found an old woman who lay moaning pitifully beside a pile of butchered bodies. Yeduza went to her side and pressed a calabash of water to her lips.

The old woman's eyes cleared after she had drunk thirstily for some time. It was clear that she was dying; there was a deep wound in her belly. Dogo stood back, looking around uncertainly as Yeduza pillowed the old woman's grey head on her knee.

'What happened here, old woman?' Yeduza asked. 'Was it the Kikwenzi? Led by the man who calls himself Chinja?'

'I do not know their names,' the old woman whispered. 'They entered the village at dawn, spearing the people as they tried to run. Silent warriors, their faces daubed white. In a brief space, all lay dead except the young people who were dragged off. The raiders feasted on the bodies of the villagers they killed, devouring them like beasts. One speared me and left me for dead.'

'Has the Emperor not sent warriors to defend your villages?' Yeduza demanded. If Chinja's forces still raided Nago, it was Mtogo's duty to send out his army to patrol the plains.

The old woman shook her head.

'The Emperor does not concern himself with us,' she wheezed. 'It is said that he has gone mad. He remains in his city and has dismissed his general. The army is leaderless. He holds executions every day, people he blames for the raids. They say... A trader from the city said... that he is rebuilding the House of Skulls...'

Yeduza's blood ran cold.

5   *The Northern Desert*

'WHAT IS the House of Skulls?' Dogo asked, shortly after. They had dug a grave in the red earth for the old woman, whose ghost left her body with her final words. Now they were interring her. Even now, what she had said resounded within Yeduza's mind. *The House of Skulls...*

'When my lord, the Emperor Mtogo, was little more than an outlaw,' she said, after they had filled in the grave, 'Nago was ruled by an evil tyrant called Mungu-Ovu. He dwelt in Mnara, where he had a palace whose mud walls were studded with the skulls of those he had slain. Mtogo gathered a band of warriors. I was young then, a girl, and I joined them after Mungu-Ovu's leopard-warriors slew my father and mother. There was little left for me except revenge in those days.

'He began a rebellion against Mungu-Ovu. During those years, I rose from the ranks to become Mtogo's right hand warrior. We overthrew Mungu-Ovu and took over Nago. Mtogo's first act after slaying the tyrant was to demolish the House of Skulls and have the bones buried to lay their ghosts to rest.' She looked at Dogo with troubled eyes. 'What has happened to my lord, that he has reverted to the ways of the one he overthrew?'

Dogo looked compassionately at her. 'It seems that your emperor poses as great a threat as Chinja,' he said.

'I must go to him,' said Yeduza suddenly. 'I cannot waste time on this fruitless quest. It is far to the northern deserts. Many, many leagues lie between us and the lands of the Tiburi; all Nago, where the Kikwenzi roam unchecked. I must go to Mtogo and persuade him to fight back. He has lost heart now that I am not with him…'

Dogo shook his head. 'No,' he said shortly. 'What would you achieve by that? He has already tried to have you killed. And why? Because the Kikwenzi defeated you. So they would again, if you led the Nagos against them with spears and knives.'

Yeduza extended her arm, helplessly gesturing at the ransacked village. 'I cannot stand by when the Nagos are under attack!'

Dogo reached up to put his hand on her arm. 'I do not tell you to stand by,' he said. 'Chinja must be defeated before anyone is safe. Only when you have the means to slay him, and have vanquished his warriors, can you think about anything else. Chinja must die.'

Yeduza sighed, and dragged her knuckles across her brow. After a moment, she said, 'You are right, Dogo. I can achieve nothing as I am. A penniless wanderer. Why, I do not even own a horse! We must journey north as fast as we can.'

'Then let us start at once!' Dogo cried. He led her at a run from the village.

***

THE SUN beat down. The wind moaned among the sands. Yeduza licked futilely at her dry lips, and gazed at the barren sea of sand that had surrounded them since they quit the ravaged lands of Nago. She propped her assegai in the crook of her arm, shaded her eyes against the glare, and scanned the horizon.

They had had a long, dangerous journey across an empire plunged into anarchy. At many points along the way, Yeduza had thought she would never see the sands of the northern desert. Now they stretched around her on every side, and she realised how hard it would be to find wandering nomads in such a bleak and empty land.

She licked her lips again, and heard a dry croak from Dogo. Looking down, she saw him shaking the calabash of water they had filled at the last waterhole. He caught her gaze and shook his head.

'We need water.'

Silently, Yeduza scanned the horizon another time; the pygmy was right, water was their first priority. Barbarians, and the salvation of Nago, would have to come second. They could not save the empire if they died of thirst. Her eyes settled on something, a depression in the sands, a *wadi*. Could they find water there? They might have to dig, but the precious drops would be all that stood between them and slow, lingering death. She indicated the *wadi* to Dogo.

'We might find water there,' she said, and was shocked by the way that her voice cracked, like a dry, dusty bone.

Dogo nodded, panting like a dog. 'I know little of these northern lands,' he said. 'I was here only briefly with the Kikwenzi. But I trust you.'

As she limped beside him across the baking sands towards the distant *wadi*, Yeduza looked guiltily at her companion. He had great faith in her, this loyal little man from the forest, but her fund of desert lore was meagre. She could not guarantee that the dried-up riverbed towards which they were walking would yield any water. No vegetation grew along its banks. But she could not see any plants anywhere among the sands that surrounded them.

They reached the *wadi*. Yeduza began to dig using her assegai. Dogo aided her with his blowpipe, and then his bare hands.

Sand gave way to sand, and more sand, dry sand that trickled back into the pit they dug. Now the wind that had been moaning across the dunes began to pick up, screaming and wailing as it hurtled across the desert. Yeduza looked up to see a sandstorm towering on the skyline like a vengeful spirit of the desert. It began to whirl towards them.

She flung down her assegai and turned urgently to Dogo.

'A storm!' she mouthed, pointing towards the whirlwind that was now so loud her words were inaudible. 'We need shelter!'

Dogo pointed towards the hole they had dug, seized her hand, and drew her down into it. The storm hit them, and stinging grains of sand were everywhere, a swirling chaos in which Yeduza, crouched in the pit, lost all sense of reality. As the storm reached its height, she lost consciousness.

***

A BOOT in her ribs stirred her, shocked her back into awareness. Her eyes were gummed together but she could hear that the storm was gone. The desert was silent except for a muted sound of voices and a stench of animals.

A voice snapped something in a foreign tongue, and the boot thudded into her ribs again. She opened her eyes to be confronted by a close-up view of sand. Weakly, she moved her head to one side, and saw a tall man glaring down at her, clad in white robes that left his face veiled except his burning, hawkish eyes. Behind him was a monstrosity Yeduza recognised dimly as a camel. She blinked and focussed on the thing the man carried nonchalantly in his right hand; a long iron object with an ornately carved wooden stock. A musket!

She had found the barbarians.

She tried to rise, and found that her arms would not obey her. Angrily, she tore at them, to discover she was bound. In her struggle, which the man watched with eyes as pitiless as the desert sun, she glimpsed her watchers' companions. More nomads, more camels - and a long coffle of slaves, their wrists bound to wooden poles. She had been found by slavers.

The barbarian looming over her produced a long whip and again gestured to her to rise. He barked an order in what Yeduza presumed to be his own tongue, then followed it by commands in other languages. Finally, Yeduza caught a word in Bengue, which she spoke but little.

'Up!' the barbarian was barking. 'Rise, wool-head! Rise, ape!'

Yeduza gritted her teeth. She would get up, certainly, if only to teach this stinking cameleer what happened to those who insulted an Amazon of Nago. She struggled to her knees, glowering; off-balance with her bound hands, feeling pain from her lame leg. The Tiburi slaver watched in silence.

Finally, Yeduza rose to her feet, and stood before the Tiburi, her arms still bound. He handed his musket to another slaver, and came closer to her. She curled her lip at the smell of his unwashed body.

'Slave!' he snapped. 'You - slave now! Get in coffle!' He indicated the line of slaves with a jerk of his head.

Yeduza looked at him, her eyes full of hate. She drew back her head and spat in his face.

He jerked back, and glared at her, incensed. He rushed towards her, whip upraised, and she lifted her good leg and kicked him in the belly. He fell back on the sands as his fellow barbarians laughed. Yeduza, off-balance again, toppled to the ground nearby.

Weakly, she got to her knees again, only to see the barbarian rise. He kicked her in the face and she went back down. Then he was on top of her, tearing at her clothes. She fought to throw him off but he had her pinioned. He gripped her tunic and yanked it down, with a cruel grin of satisfaction. Suddenly, his eyes widened, and he half rose.

A dart jutted from his neck. With a confused, querulous moan, he slumped across her body.

Angrily, Yeduza thrust the limp body to one side with her leg. Again, she got to her feet and stood there swaying slightly. What had happened? She looked at the surrounding slavers, who regarded their dead chief in bafflement. She looked down at the corpse and her eyes fixed on the dart. Scanning the dunes surrounding them, she thought she saw a small, black figure duck into cover. She smiled slowly, then she turned to the Tiburi.

'Set me free!' she shouted in Bengue. 'Cut my bonds - or you will all die as did your leader! I came here to trade, not to be treated as a slave!'

'Who are you, then?' Another barbarian stepped forward, the one who had taken the chieftain's musket. He pulled down his veil to reveal a pale, youthful face with a cynical smile and laughing, dancing eyes. 'What do you wish to trade?'

'Free me, and then we can talk,' Yeduza replied. The barbarian shrugged, shouldered the two muskets, and produced an ornate, curved-bladed dagger. He crossed to her side and slashed her bonds. Yeduza stretched her arms then hurriedly replaced her tunic. She searched the surrounding sands for her shield and assegai, but saw no sign of them.

'I am Assouad,' the youth declared. He indicated the dead chieftain. 'Now that Hagal is dead by your sorcery, I succeed him as leader of the caravan. You have done us a favour - none of us liked him; he was greedy, always kept the best prizes for himself. You speak of trade, black witch. What do you wish to buy? What do you have to offer?' His eyes flicked up and down her scornfully.

Yeduza's mind raced. Throughout the journey, she had been anticipating this moment, this question. What did she have to trade? She no longer even had the horse, the assegai, or the shield that were all she had taken with her when she fled Mnara.

'Let me tell you what I want,' she said. 'My land is Nago. I am captain of the Emperor's Guard. My country is under attack from warriors who use sorcery to make themselves invulnerable to spears or swords. I have learnt that muskets can kill them. I wish to buy a musket so that I can slay their leader, Chinja.'

'Impossible,' said Assouad. 'We are forbidden to sell muskets to your folk. Had you wool-heads the means to make them, we free people of the desert would lose our edge over you. We do not have a deal.'

Yeduza snarled. 'Listen to me, camel offal,' she said, 'I have travelled far to trade. Listen to me, or my familiar spirit' - she raised her voice in the hopes that Dogo would hear behind his sand dune - 'will strike you down!'

Assouad turned back, his eyes flickering towards Hagal's stiffening corpse. 'You expect me to trade under duress?' he demanded. 'There's such a thing as good will, woman.'

'My name is Yeduza,' she hissed. 'You will call me "Yeduza" or "my lady". You will not call me "wool-head", or "ape", and certainly, you will not call me "woman." I am an Amazon of Nago, and you will treat me as my rank demands. Or else my…'

'…familiar spirit will strike me dead, yes. I heard you the first time,' Assouad replied. 'From which I can only conclude you are a witch. Why not use your black sorcery to fight this Chinja?'

Yeduza gritted her teeth. 'I have told you what I want,' she said. 'I want a musket.'

Assouad folded his arms. 'I'll consider it,' he said. 'But what do you have to offer in return? You can strike me dead, but will your familiar spirit stop the bullets of my men as they sink into your carcass?' He studied her face. 'I thought as not. Then what do you have to trade?'

'*The plunder of the Kikwenzi!*'

Yeduza looked up in amazement to see Dogo racing down the dune towards them. The barbarians whirled round. Even the cowed slaves looked on in amusement as Dogo rushed to Yeduza's side.

'So this is your familiar spirit,' said Assouad with a laugh. 'I could get a good price for a dwarf like him, in the stone cities beyond the desert.' Yeduza ignored him, looking down at her pygmy friend.

'I was with the Kikwenzi when they looted the caravan that carried the gold tribute from the miners of the south to the kingdom of Habesh, in the eastern mountains,' Dogo told Assouad. 'They

43

have it still.' He turned to Yeduza. 'Offer them that in return for their aid.'

Yeduza smiled. 'You hear that, Assouad?' she said. 'Aid us, and we will let you take your pick of the Kikwenzi's plunder. They have been raiding for many years. You are welcome to as much as you wish.'

Assouad's eyes were wide with greed. 'The gold of Habesh...' he breathed. 'Woman, it is a done deal. We will come with you. We will fight for you. It is against our code to let wool-heads buy muskets, but for the promise of the gold of Habesh, I will give you this.' He handed her the musket that had belonged to Hagal. Yeduza took it eagerly, and examined the weapon.

'Will you instruct me in its use?' she demanded.

Assouad laughed. 'Lady, you strike a hard bargain,' he said. 'But for even a chance at so much gold, I will do even that.' He glanced at the huddled form at their feet. 'And you might as well take Hagal's camel. He won't need it. Come, let us make haste. Where is this Chinja?'

Yeduza shouldered the musket, and limped to Hagal's camel, Dogo following. Before she mounted the ugly-looking beast, she turned to Assouad.

'One last condition,' she said. The barbarian sighed.

'What now, wo... my lady?'

Yeduza indicated the slaves. 'Set them free when we reach Nago.'

Assouad flung up his hands in anger. Then he laughed suddenly. 'This had

better be worth it,' he said. He mounted his camel.

Slowly, the caravan moved on its way, leaving behind it the stiffening body of Hagal, motionless in the desert sands. As the barbarians and their companions crested the brow of the dunes, the vultures swooped down.

6   The Dark One

'BEYOND THOSE trees is the Kikwenzi camp,' Dogo whispered, pointing towards the collection of baobabs that clustered on the skyline. 'I crept as close as I could. Their guards did not see me, the dull-witted fools. The spell that controls them makes them useless as sentries.

'There is a palisade within which the Kikwenzi have pitched their tents. In the centre of the compound is a large tent, topped by the skull of a gazelle. That must be Chinja's tent. Elsewhere the Kikwenzi loll about, or clean weapons, or go about menial tasks. From Chinja's tent, I caught the sound of cruel laughter, and cries for mercy. They have captives.'

'Good work,' said Yeduza from her camel. 'We shall...'

Assouad leaned forward. 'I think this is where my men come in,' he said. 'We shall set about this like any slave raid. Approach rapidly, and begin shooting once we are among them. If what you say about this sorcerer is true, all we need do is reach the tent and kill him, and then the spell will be broken. Without him, his horde will be easy to round up.'

Yeduza frowned at the barbarian. 'Remember that this is not a slave raid,' she said firmly. 'These people have laboured under Chinja's spell. They may have committed terrible crimes. But they are Nago, and I will see them free - from Chinja's spell, or your slavery.'

Assouad tossed his head back in annoyance. 'What profit will we see on this venture?' he demanded.

'Do not forget the treasure of Habesh,' Dogo reminded him. Assouad looked down at the little man, and shrugged. He turned in his saddle and rapped out a string of orders to his men.

They all dismounted, leaving the camels in the care of two youths, loaded their muskets with gunpowder and shot, rammed it down, and began to advance towards the trees. Yeduza joined them, her loaded musket over her shoulder, Dogo trotting at her heels.

They passed through the trees and Yeduza saw the palisade rising before them, its stakes dark against the blue sky. Several Kikwenzi squatted in the entrance, beyond which a confusion of tents and figures was visible. Two Kikwenzi rose as the nomads marched towards them. Assouad and another barbarian opened fire.

The shots rang out loud and fierce, a roar of thunder that seemed to ram Yeduza's ears into her skull. Despite the training she had received during the journey, she was still not used to the sheer noise.

The two Kikwenzi collapsed to the red earth, like broken dolls. Fleetingly, Yeduza remembered another time, an innocent time many years before, playing with her dolls in the earth outside her father's house. Those days were long gone. The remaining guards

rose, their assegais at the ready. More Tiburi shot them down.

Assouad motioned to those of his men who had not yet fired. 'In!' he shouted. 'Into the compound!'

He began to reload his musket. Yeduza and Dogo joined the other barbarians as they flooded through the gateway, firing as they came. Kikwenzi fell, to litter the compound in huddled heaps. The acrid tang of the gunpowder and its white clouds filled the air. Kikwenzi shambled back and forth.

Assouad and the rest rushed in as the first line reloaded. Assouad levelled his musket. Yeduza saw a Kikwenzi nearby with a throwing knife, poised to fling it at the nomad leader. She levelled her musket, not yet fired, pulled the trigger, and blew the man's chest away.

Shots cracked out from the barbarians. More Kikwenzi fell. Yeduza felt her gorge rise. It was a massacre, no better than a Kikwenzi attack. And these poor fools were under Chinja's spell.

'Wait!' she screamed at Assouad. 'We must press forward! Kill Chinja!'

Assouad shook his head. 'We must settle these wool-heads first!' he roared, his eyes alight with unholy glee. He put his musket to his shoulder and fired. An advancing Kikwenzi warrior dropped writhing to the earth.

Yeduza turned to Dogo urgently. 'Where is Chinja's tent?' she demanded. Dogo pointed. Through the acrid, spicy clouds of gunsmoke, Yeduza caught a glimpse of a large tent on the far side of the compound. She clapped the pygmy on the shoulder, and hurriedly loaded her musket. The barbarians were still firing into the crowd of Kikwenzi. Two barbarians had fallen to assegais or throwing knives. The moment that Yeduza had rammed down her shot, she shouldered her musket and limped quickly forward.

'Where are you going?' Assouad shouted at her vanishing figure. Dogo trotted hurriedly after her.

Three Kikwenzi came forward to meet her, wicked-looking blades glinting in their hands. She swung the musket like a club, beat the warriors back, then raced on through the smoke and the noise. She came out into an open area. At the far end was Chinja's tent. Standing before it, watching the barbarian attack with cold eyes, was Chinja and a group of tall warriors, each one with his face daubed white.

Chinja's serpent eyes widened as he saw Yeduza step out into the open space. He pointed a trembling finger at her. 'Kill her!' he shouted. Two large Kikwenzi warriors lumbered towards her, assegais raised. Cursing, she tried to dodge aside. Dogo put his blowpipe to his lips and suddenly a dart was projecting from the left-hand warrior's neck. The Kikwenzi felt at it with annoyance, then brushed it away. Dogo turned to run, and the other Kikwenzi seized him, lifting him high to dash him to the ground. Yeduza turned, and opened fire.

The shot knocked the Kikwenzi against a nearby tent, which collapsed under his weight. Dogo rolled free, and looked up. Yeduza still held the smoking musket, but her face was pale. At a footfall, she hobbled round.

Chinja and his warriors stood before her. Yeduza's heart sank. She had no time to reload the musket. She reversed it to use it as a club again. Dogo crept to her side as the Kikwenzi encircled them.

'You return…' Chinja boomed. 'With new knowledge, new weapons. You are dangerous, woman of the Nago. You will make an excellent warrior for my cause. My sorcery will rid your mind of these foolish thoughts of defending your empire, replace them with nothing but the desire to kill, kill, kill again - in my name! To lay Nago waste, until this mighty, tottering empire is no more, and a dozen warring tribes squabbling over what little remains - each spurred on by conflicting dreams of empire - is all there will be to tell those who come after what once was.'

His serpent eyes glittered as he held her in their spell. Her arms went limp, the musket that could have killed him dropped to the red earth. With an immense effort of will, she forced herself to speak.

'Why?' she moaned. 'Why do you wish to destroy us?' Even now, she could feel his mesmerising gaze at work, feel a desire to be nothing more than his slave. She dropped to her knees before him, looking up into his saturnine visage. 'Why?' she said again.

'Vengeance,' Chinja hissed. 'I - the spirit that moves this feeble frame - seek revenge upon Nago; upon Mtogo, for the woes he worked me. And you were his Amazon. But you shall bring about his death. You will work my revenge… '

A shot rang out. In the instant before Chinja's tall body collapsed, his chest holed by a bullet, Yeduza saw his serpent gaze gone entirely, replaced by frightened, wholly human eyes. Then a corpse thudded to the ground before her.

7   The Way Back

YEDUZA TURNED to see Assouad and his fellow nomads standing in the gap between the tents. Assouad was lowering his still smoking musket. All around them, Kikwenzi stood motionless, faces blank. As Yeduza returned her attention to Chinja's motionless corpse, the Kikwenzi slowly seemed to awaken, as if from deep sleep, rubbing at their eyes and looking in doubt and uncertainty at each other.

'I told you to wait until we had killed the Kikwenzi, woman!' Assouad blazed. He reloaded his musket and aimed it directly at the nearest warrior.

Yeduza looked at him. 'They pose no threat now.' As Assouad's finger tightened on the trigger, she brought her arm upwards, knocking the barrel away. The shot headed for the distant trees and a pair of vultures leapt up, squawking in dismay. Assouad glared at her.

'Where is the treasure, then?' he demanded. 'Pygmy - where is it?'

Dogo nodded towards the large tent. 'That is where Chinja kept all his plunder.'

Assouad nodded coldly. He beckoned to his men, and they forced their way through the mass of bewildered Kikwenzi towards the tent. Yeduza and Dogo followed behind them.

Assouad disappeared inside the tent. Shortly after, Yeduza heard a cry, and then the barbarian returned, dragging three Nago girls with him. He flung them down on the packed earth with a grin, and spoke to his men. He caught sight of Yeduza's eye.

'There's wealth aplenty in here,' he laughed. 'Black gold as well.' He seized one girl roughly by her chin, and ran a caressing hand down her face.

Yeduza's eyes widened. 'Princess Walata!' she exclaimed. 'How come you here?'

The girl drew back from Assouad's rough grasp and looked up at Yeduza.

'General Yeduza?' she asked softly. 'Have you joined our enemies?'

Yeduza shook her head. 'I have liberated you,' she said.

'With my aid!' Assouad broke in. 'We had a deal, woman. I killed Chinja. Now his loot is mine. Come here, girl.'

Yeduza thrust herself forward. 'No!' she said. 'This was not in the deal. You can take the gold of Habesh. But this is Walata, daughter of Mtogo, Princess of Nago.'

'A wool-head princess will fetch a fair price on a northern slave-block,' the barbarian muttered rebelliously, but he turned away and led his men inside the large tent. As Yeduza spoke to the Princess and her two handmaidens, she could hear the barbarians ransacking the tent.

'How come you here, my princess?' she asked. 'Does your father know you were captives?'

Blood Brains and Bullets

Blood, Brains and Bullets is Book One of the new Blood, Brains and Bullets series by Sean Liebling. It starts on Day One of the Outbreak and continues through the first seven full days after its apocalyptic climax.

Jay has started his daily routine as a single father of three, when the news hits of massive deaths— then reanimations—from the vaccine distributed by the government to combat the super-flu virus that has been sweeping the globe. For Jay, it's irritating because it interrupts his normal comedic attempts at nailing every sweet piece of ass in the area. Being a survivalist means he has a lot of 'stuff', as you can never have too much, and before he can even take shelter in his homemade retreat to ride out the apocalypse, friends start showing up who need his help. Before he knows it, he's forced into the unenviable position of assuming leadership over his community, or what's left of it, and fighting on multiple fronts against the forces of the evil undead, neighboring marauders, and assassins of a Shadow Government with a secret, 200-year-old New World Order Eugenics plan. Of course, that plan of theirs doesn't include him and his, so this Marine does what all Marines do best: He kicks ass without bothering to take names, and along the way he happens to fall into the clutches of a girl or three. Women can be very demanding – even during a Zombie Apocalypse!

Legacy of the Living

Jay and the other Newaygo survivors must survive the influx of undead as well as the attacks by the Shadow Government. But as a Marine, Jay doesn't plan on merely surviving-he will take this battle to them! This series is a testament to what good men can do, when doing nothing simply isn't an option! Book Two continues on, beginning with the aftermath of a devastating zombie attack. As the town mourns the loss of many of their near and dear ones, Jay and his military personnel are faced with the chilling discovery that the zombies have evolved—have become even more clever and cunning. And they seem to be focusing their attacks on the children of the survivors!

AVAILABLE FROM AMAZON.COM

About: Sean Liebling

Sean's books are about HOPE! Yet not only hope but also about self-sacrifice for fellow man/woman/child and protection of the innocent. He believes in God, Country and Patriotism. Sean writes a strong dose of 'punch in your gut', non-stop fighting action accompanied by 100% intolerance for racism or hatred of alternate lifestyle living. By the same token he is fairly conservative in most other areas of his life. Not an oxymoron, just common sense. Sean also writes with realism – as in how it may likely be. Many will disagree and Sean enjoys the discourse.

Sean served twice in the USMC who incarcerated him in Beirut, Iraq, Panama, Somalia, and a few other places until he was barely discharged for good behavior. Currently the owner of a few businesses that are actually making money in this bad economy, Sean is also a licensed firearms instructor – just to keep his hand in the game.

Sean's approachable, so if you enjoyed his book and feel like dropping him a line go right ahead. He will personally respond to each and every one. Sean's met a great many of his fans now and all were a pleasure to talk to. He also loves criticism. His feelings on that is that it helps him to become a better writer.

Walata pouted. 'My father knows nothing, cares less,' she said. 'It was because of him that I fled Mnara with my handmaidens. He had my own mother executed! I knew that I would be next. We fled into the wilderness, and there the Kikwenzi found us.' Her expression changed to one of sorrow and shame. 'They dragged us to Chinja, who made us his meanest slaves.'

Yeduza caressed her. 'Your father slew your mother?' she probed.

'He has slain many since you were banished,' Walata replied. 'The people say that the only folk he has not killed are the Kikwenzi. But in Mnara, he wades in blood. The army does his bidding in everything and the people are oppressed. And he has rebuilt the House of Skulls.'

Yeduza nodded. 'I had heard as much,' she said.

'Then why did you not come back to us?' the Princess demanded. 'The people say that only you could save us from my father's insanity. And he is insane - or possessed. Another voice speaks through his lips, another's eyes look upon this world. He is not the man I have loved throughout my life.'

'Possessed…' Yeduza whispered. She looked down at Chinja's corpse. 'Princess Walata,' she said, 'I could not aid you before now, since I was a hunted exile, alone except for my courageous companion, Dogo.' The Princess smiled at the pygmy, who bowed. 'Now I have warriors at my back, armed with new, more powerful weaponry. Mtogo's army will not prevail against them.'

'Those barbarians?' Walata asked with a shudder.

'They are valiant warriors,' Yeduza replied. 'With their aid we shall return to Mnara and speak with your father.' As she spoke, Assouad and his men swaggered back out of the tent, weighed down with gold and jewels. She beckoned to Assouad.

'Assouad,' she said. 'One last task awaits us. We must return to Mnara and end Mtogo's tyranny. He is as great a threat to the empire as ever these Kikwenzi were…'

Assouad shook his head. 'That wasn't in the deal,' he said, echoing her previous words. Yeduza's face fell. 'We have the treasure. My men fought for you. Now they are rewarded. We didn't agree to anything else.' He walked away towards the edge of the compound, followed by his men.

Yeduza hobbled after them. 'Wait!' she cried. 'Can we not strike another deal? What can I offer you? I must return to the city. Mtogo is a tyrant. He must be stopped…'

Assouad halted, and grinned. He showed her the gold that weighed him down. 'What could you possibly offer me to better this?' he said. 'With this I could buy a palace north of the desert, with slaves and houris and Mamelukes to do my every bidding. Each of my men could have their own palace. What can you possibly offer me, in your flyspeck of an empire? Mud huts? Black sluts? No, Yeduza. This adventure ends here for me.' He turned, and swaggered away.

Yeduza watched with sadness as he and his men pushed their way through the milling throng. He was crude, insulting, objectionable… But what would she do when he was gone?

Dogo joined her, and then Walata.

'Do not be so sad,' said Dogo sympathetically.

Yeduza turned on him. 'What chance do we stand against Mtogo now?' she demanded bitterly. 'His army still remains loyal. We can only end his tyranny if we have strength on our side.'

'If we need an army,' Walata said tentatively, 'look around you!'

Yeduza looked around. All she could see were the milling, confused, ex-Kikwenzi warriors. Then it struck her, and she smiled.

'Of course!' she cried.

**

THE HOST halted at the crest of the rise. Below them, like a trickle of silver across the red earth of the savannah, the Nago River wound away into the shimmering haze. Foursquare and grim, the city of Mnara stood before them.

But it was a different city from the one Yeduza had last seen. Vultures circled above it, but she saw no smoke trails. Stakes stood along its adobe ramparts, each one bearing the black shape of an impaled figure. Other bodies hung from trees that grew out in the plain. She had followed a trail of corpses on her journey across the savannah, more and more as they neared Mnara.

She looked down from her camel - Assouad had left her that much - at her forces as they arrayed themselves on either hand. Dogo sat pillion, gazing down at the great city with troubled eyes. She had grown accustomed to the presence of the little man. Now she wondered how things would turn out

once they had completed this quest. Mtogo must be stopped; he had gone mad in the face of all-powerful enemies who only Yeduza had had the means and the desire to crush. Could she nurse him back to sanity? Or would it be her painful duty to kill him, as if he was a mad dog? What then? What would happen to the Empire of Nago without its emperor?

Perhaps Walata could succeed. Yeduza had left the girl in a friendly village on the way. The beautiful princess was young and naïve, but perhaps with Yeduza's guidance she could become an empress capable of holding the empire together.

She shook her head. Enough introspection. Time to stop thinking and to seek some form of resolution. There was no sign of resistance from the army of Nago. She turned to the Kikwenzi commanders and urged them on with a gesture. Then her camel trotted forward, carrying Dogo and her at their head.

They crossed the plain, inching towards those towering brown walls, their advance seen only by the blind eyes of the impaled corpses that lined the ramparts, and the feasting vultures that flapped off in anger as they came ever closer. Yeduza found her breath coming in short pants. Anticipation constricted her chest. The sun glowered down from a sky the colour of cobalt.

At last, the ebon east gate of Mnara rose before them. A stake stood on either side, and Yeduza saw to her horror that the figures impaled upon them were members of Mtogo's Amazon Guard, women she might have recognised from parades, might have sat with at feasts; but their faces were gone, picked clean by the vultures that still circled overhead.

'Mtogo's guards are not vigilant,' Dogo murmured. Yeduza paid him no heed, but turned to one of her commanders, a tall, burly man named Pambazuko.

'Take your warriors and scout ahead,' she commanded. 'We must learn the reason for this silent welcome.'

He nodded stiffly, and went to his men. Shortly after, they were advancing on the gate. After briefly examining the impaled figures, Pambazuko led the men into the shadow of the city beyond. Rapidly, it swallowed them up.

Yeduza and her host stood silently in the glare of the sun. Seconds passed, and the only sound was a muted whisper of wind as it stirred the withered grasses. Out of the corner of her eye, Yeduza thought she saw a cloud of dust moving along the northern horizon. She peered towards it uncertainly. It resembled the dust trail created by a group of riders. What riders could be out there now? Were they Mtogo's forces? Should she alert her forces? What did it portend?

In this eerie silence, anything seemed like an omen of doom.

'My lady?'

She turned in her saddle to see that Pambazuko had returned. He stood looking up at her, his face grim.

'Much of the city is deserted; at least the streets are. We think that the citizens might be hiding in their houses. But we met no resistance. All was silent, except we could hear the sound of chanting and shouting from the middle of the city.'

Yeduza listened intently. Pambazuko was a Bengue, and he had never seen Mnara before he had been dragged off to fight for Chinja. The centre of the city - that would be the direction of the palace. Or where the palace had once stood…

She made a decision. Beckoning her commanders to her, she explained.

'I will take a small party of warriors, and we shall issue into the city. At the first signs of trouble, advance after us in force. It seems that Mtogo has left all his defences down. Perhaps it is a trap. Perhaps not. We shall see. Meanwhile, I shall leave Dogo with you to represent me.'

There was some muttering as she said this, and Dogo himself looked anxious. But Yeduza was sure that she could leave the host in his hands. He had proved himself a capable companion in the time they had been together.

She gathered a picked force of thirty warriors, and together they advanced towards the gates. The stink of corruption made Yeduza gag as they came closer to the impaled corpses, both at the gate and along the ramparts. Yeduza looked back one last time, to see Dogo standing among the tall commanders.

In the distance, the cloud of dust seemed to be drawing closer. One thing at a time, she told herself. Her forces were large enough to fend off any surprise attack, assuming her imagination had not got the better of her. Then they were past the gates, and entering the city.

The city was deserted, as Pambazuko had said. Yeduza led her warriors cautiously past cracked adobe walls, along streets where sand lay in drifts, coming closer and closer to the centre, where the palace had once stood. She could see no sign of its high roofs from here. Had Mtogo destroyed it?

At last, without any resistance, Yeduza and her warriors came out into the square at the centre of Mnara, where the palace had once stood. Her heart hammered in her ears as she saw the great, grisly building that had replaced it.

Human skulls lined its every surface. It had been built almost entirely of skulls, cemented together with adobe. A great archway of skulls led into the dark interior. Even the pavement before it comprised of skulls. An altar stood beneath the arch, and here a small group presided over a scene of horror.

Two women held a struggling youth down over the altar. Towering over them was a horrific figure. Yeduza stared in sick, pitying horror as she recognised it as her erstwhile emperor, Mtogo.

When last she had seen him, his eyes had been dull, his muscular body run to seed. Now all his fat had vanished, and his frame was gaunt and withered, but his eyes glared from his skull-like face... like the eyes of a serpent.

As he raised a knife above him to disembowel the writhing figure the two women pinioned, those serpent eyes, so strangely familiar, fixed on her own, and she felt a thrill of horrified, impossible recognition.

Mtogo dropped the knife, and it fell with a clatter on the pavement of skulls. He grinned, and stepped round the altar, leaving the sacrifice in the hands of his Amazons, and halted a few metres from Yeduza's motionless, paralysed form.

'You return to dog me once more,' he boomed, and even his voice seemed wrong. 'Will you try to kill me, as you did last time?'

Yeduza stirred, filled with righteous wrath.

'I made no attempt to kill you,' she blazed. 'You would have killed me, because the Kikwenzi defeated me. After my many years of service...'

'You have joined the Kikwenzi now,' the Emperor said, indicating her companions.

'I freed them!' Yeduza replied. 'I brought about Chinja's downfall. Now I come to you, to beg you - end this killing! What has happened to Nago; what has happened to you, my lord? What has brought you to this?'

Those snake-like eyes glittered, naggingly familiar. 'I - the spirit that moves this feeble frame - seek revenge on Nago; upon Mtogo, for the woes he worked me. And you were his Amazon. But you shall bring about his death. You will work my revenge... '

Yeduza shivered in horror to hear those words; the same words she had heard from Chinja, his final words. It was as if they were continuing the same conversation.

'Who are you?' she whispered. 'What spirit? Are you not Emperor Mtogo?'

'I infiltrated his dreams, spoke to him in the dark spaces of his mind,' the man said. 'Even as I animated Chinja, and held his warriors under my spell, I worked upon Mtogo himself. When you slew Chinja, I put an end to my whisperings, and instead came to live in Mtogo's heart. Your Emperor is gone. Only I remain - Mungu-Ovu!'

Yeduza's scalp crawled as those eyes blazed down at her. With a supreme effort of will, she lifted her assegai and plunged it into his naked chest.

He laughed as the blade passed through him as if he were no more than a phantom. 'You tried that before,' he taunted her. 'Where are your barbarian allies now? Where are your weapons of subtle craft? I am a sorcerer. I control this land, this realm, as I did in life. I control the Emperor, and through him I will destroy the Empire that spurned me!' He clicked his fingers. 'Take her to the altar!'

Yeduza was horrified as two Kikwenzi stepped forward to take her arms. She struggled and fought and damned them as traitors as they dragged her across the skull-pavement towards the altar where Mtogo - no, Mungu-Ovu! - stood now, his knife in his hands again.

'One space remains in my house of skulls,' he said. 'I had hoped to fill it with the braincase of this oaf,' - he indicated the youth still struggling in the two women's arms - 'but the skull of Mtogo's general will be more fitting.'

The two Kikwenzi bent Yeduza over the altar. Their faces were blank, as if she had never freed them from their slavery. Now Mungu-Ovu lifted the knife over her breast, ready to plunge it in. For a moment, all was silent. Yeduza struggled feebly in the iron grip of the Kikwenzi, knowing that she was close to the end.

A shot rang out across the courtyard. Yeduza's eyes widened as she saw a small hole appear in Mungu-Ovu's forehead. Blood dribbled from it. His eyes rolled upwards in their sockets. The knife clattered down on the skull pavement a second time. Slowly, like a toppled tree, the body collapsed.

As if waking from a dream, the two Kikwenzi stared down at Yeduza. They let go of her immediately, and she drew herself up. Then she turned.

Familiar figures stood at the edge of the courtyard. Smoke drifted up from the barrel of Assouad's musket. Behind him, his warriors sat upon camelback, watching the scene with impassive faces. At Assouad's side stood Dogo, and the rest of the Kikwenzi commanders were behind them.

Assouad swaggered forwards. Yeduza stared down at the skulls at her feet and was silent.

'You thought I'd left you to it, eh?' he laughed. 'I couldn't. All that gold - well, it will set me up for life. But I could never settle down in a palace in the north. Not now. Not since I have known you. You are not like other women, Yeduza. Not like the soft, simpering houris north of the desert, or even the strong, earthy women of the Tiburi. You are like no one I have ever met. So I thought I would ride back and join you. Good thing I did. Your Emperor had gone mad, I see. You were in danger. I saved you.

'You're very quiet. Didn't you want me to help you? Say something! Look at me, woman! Look at me!'

Dogo tugged at Assouad's arm, and he looked down at the pygmy.

'Yeduza is tired,' the little man said softly, his face compassionate. 'Leave

53

her be for now. We have celebrations to prepare.'

Unwillingly, Assouad allowed the pygmy to lead him away. As the warriors moved into the city *en masse*, he looked over his shoulder one last time at Yeduza as she stood there in the shadows. Then he and the others filed from the courtyard. Soon sounds of jubilation were audible from the streets outside.

In the silence of the House of Skulls, Yeduza's face lifted. Serpent eyes glittered with hate.

The eyes of Mungu-Ovu.

ABOUT THE AUTHOR

Gavin Chappell was raised by a pack of friendly cats in suburban England and lives near Liverpool. After studying English at the University of Wales, he went on to work in leisure before drifting into teaching where he spent the next decade trying to drift out again. He is now editor of *Schlock! Webzine*.

THE CAVES OF MARS
Gregory KH Bryant

Previously in "The Caves of Mars":

Our hero, Grae-don, awakens from a timeless unconsciousness to find himself in a strange world of an infinite golden ocean and ceaseless amber skies.

Having no knowledge of who or what he is, and drifting for days, he comes at last upon the island city called Pella'mir, where he is taken in by the minions of the heartless scientist Jor-Taq, and taught to speak, read and write by Jor-Taq's slaves, for purposes yet unknown.

Chapter 2: My Education Continues

HORATH LED me through a series of long and narrow corridors illumined by the yellow rectangles of light of lamps set into the red stone walls. He strode arrogantly before me, while his escort, my guard, followed behind.

We marched in silence. Horath uttered not a word, and I took these moments to examine him most closely. He stood perhaps a head taller than me, and his body was heavy with muscles. His chest was broad and his waist was narrow. He let his arms swing freely at his sides, and I saw that his hands were huge and callused. Horath swaggered when he walked, and every fibre of his body bespoke arrogance and cruelty.

I'd noticed the smirk of smug self-satisfaction on his face before. I had already learned to hate the man. Now, I compared his visage with his body and carriage, and in those moments walking behind him, I came to despise him completely.

Seeking to annoy him, I asked, "What is a koraph?" I already knew, of course. Shala and Haia had given me a very thorough education, but I sensed it would irritate him to answer the question, impertinently asked, but disguised as naïve. And it did.

"Shut up!" he said, without turning. One of the guards behind gave me a cuff at the back of the head with the pommel of his sword.

The blow was hard, but not sufficient to harm me. But I saw that Horath was indeed annoyed, and that gave me some satisfaction.

We climbed several steep stairways, passing a number of chambers, all of them dark, and then down a winding passage to a black door that was securely bolted. Horath rapped on the door with his knuckles, and a small portal opened, revealing the face of another guard.

He looked past Horath to scrutinize my face. After several moments, he demanded, "Is this the one?"

"It is he," Horath said.

"Then bring him inside. You and this one. The others wait without."

We stepped into a small anteroom and waited while the guard securely bolted the door. Then, once that was locked, he stepped to a door on the opposite wall and opened it.

"Wait here," he said, and he disappeared behind the door.

Now Horath turned to glower at me. "You are about to enter the presence of Jor-Taq. Keep a respectful tongue, koraph, or I'll cut it out and feed it to you."

"As you say," I replied.

Without a word, Horath punched me in the head.

"Speak when you're told to, slave!" he spat, by way of explanation.

I glared at him in silence, and he read the expression on my face. He laughed.

"If you think you can, then do it now, koraph!" He raised his fist and held it before my nose.

"Ha! I thought so," he said, when I made no move. "You're not the first man to look at me like that. Many men have thought to kill me. Some have even tried. Ha, ha, ha!"

Obviously Horath gave himself much amusement.

The door opened suddenly, and the guard stepped in with a quick gesture.

"Do not keep Jor-Taq waiting," he said. "Nor seek to impose upon him, or it will go not well for you." That last comment was directed at me.

Horath ushered me forward, where we found Jor-Taq at table, having just finished his supper. A girl was removing the crockery, and she caught my eye, for she was different from all others I had seen here.

She was petite, almost tiny, you might say. Her head came no higher than my shoulder. But what struck me first about her was her golden hair, which she wore loosely and cut rather short and curled about her ears. All the others I had seen to this moment had hair that was black, straight and glossy.

And then I noticed her complexion. Her skin was light, like mine, rather pinkish in tone, and not at all of the golden sheen of all the others I had met here. That surprised me, and because we shared a strange complexion, I felt a sudden affinity toward her, and a sense of a strange familiarity.

Were we kindred, in this place? Were there other places, other worlds, other lives where our paths may have crossed before this moment? I do not know. To this day I do not know. All I can say is that at that moment when I first laid eyes on her, it with was with a sense of strange recognition, all unexplainable.

And then I saw her eyes, and they were an astonishment, for they were blue, an unheard of blue. In a world where everyone's eyes were green, or black, or – in my case, brown – blue eyes were undreamed of. And I saw that they were eyes that were meant to be happy, always smiling, often laughing, eyes of good-humour and gentle friendship. She should not be in a dismal place, such as this. She should not be subjected to serving these cold and heartless creatures, treated with endless discourtesies. Whoever she was, she had a place in the world, and this was not it.

She wore only a tiny cloth wrapped about her loins. It was not of leather, but of white fabric, stained with the soil and discoloration of the menial tasks she served. About her neck was a collar, and this studded with a ring in the back. Later, I learned, that collar was for the convenience of her keepers, that they may use it to chain her securely when her guards were not present.

She never looked up from her tasks, but moved silently through the room, removing the cutlery and crockery from the table of Jor-Taq, and then swiftly removing herself from his presence.

But I caught fleeting glimpses of her eyes, glances that bespoke a quick mind and an intelligence that was attentive to her environment. This girl, I sensed, was more intelligent than those who presumed to be her keepers.

She was – I realized, of a sudden – more dangerous to them than they were to her.

But Jor-Taq was oblivious. He glared at me over the table as Horath ushered me forward, ignoring the girl completely.

She finished her task, and then she was gone, leaving me alone in the room with Jor-Taq and Horath.

Jor-Taq glared at me for several long moments saying nothing. The he rose from his table and walked up to me, hunched with age, and peering up at my face.

"Pale skin," he remarked, more to himself than to me. "Yellow hair. Brown eyes."

He hobbled a full circle around me, poking at me with his gnarled fingers and muttering. Then he came to face me once again, squinting with ill-temper.

"Who are you?" he demanded.

"I don't know. Shala and Haia call me Grae-don." "You don't know?" he demanded.

"No."

"They tell me you walked in from the sea. Is that true?"

"Yes," I answered, shrugging my shoulders, helplessly.

"And where do you come from?"

"The sea, I suppose. I remember nothing, but drifting for days and days, and then I saw the islands."

"We have seen some few like you before," Jor-Taq mused. "They claim to come from the southern seas. Do you know of these?"

"No. I only know what Shala and Haia have taught me."

Turning abruptly to Horath, Jor-Taq demanded, "What do you think? Is this man lying?"

"I think he does not have the intelligence to lie," Horath answered with a sneer. "He is very stupid."

"Is that right? Jor-Taq asked me, a supercilious smile touching his lips. "Are you stupid?"

"It took him long to learn to speak," Horath put in. "Longer than even a child."

"If you say I am stupid, then I must be," I answered. "I know almost nothing."

"Good. Good," Jor-Taq replied. "No, I do not believe you are lying to me, stupid one. I can tell a liar. Don't ever try. I will have you put to death, if ever you lie to me."

"I will not lie to you," I lied.

"Good. See to it you don't. Don't even think a lie when I am about."

Jor-Taq led Horath away to the other side of the room and they huddled together in close and whispered conversation for several moments. At last they came to an agreement between them, and returned to me.

"You will go with Horath now. He will see to your training."

"What of Shala and Haia? Will they not teach me anymore?"

Horath reached out and slapped me hard, so hard that I fell sprawling upon the floor. Jor-Taq simply smirked.

"Do not question Jor-Taq, slave! Do what you are told, and be grateful for it!" And then he stepped forward to kick me, while I was still down, but I was too quick for him. Instantly I was on my feet again.

His foot came within an inch of my nose. Without thinking, I grabbed it by the heel tightly in both of my hands, and raised it suddenly to the level of my shoulder. Instantly, Horath's face was ridiculous with dismay.

With his right foot gripped firmly in my hands, and raised high, he was suddenly helpless. He could not strike me with his fists, which failed uselessly in the air, and his attention was otherwise wholly engaged with bouncing madly on his left foot, as he strove to keep his balance.

Jor-Taq laughed out loud, delighted at the fearsome Horath's suddenly silly figure. Horath's face was contorted with anger and he burned orange with livid, impotent, rage.

For an instant, I was as surprised at the result of my impulsive act as he was, but only for an instant. Goaded on by Jor-Taq's merriment, I dragged Horath in circles about the room by his upraised foot, while he shouted, sputtered and cursed, hopping absurdly to keep from falling.

A stream of obscenities spewed from his mouth, words too foul for me to countenance, but the threats were most clear.

"I'll cut your filthy throat!" he bellowed. "I'll gut you, I'll slice your manhood from you and shove it down your neck until you choke, you stinking *kra*[1]-gorging koraph!"

Jor-Taq, laughing uproariously, interjected, "You'll do nothing of the sort. This Grae-don amuses me. You will leave him unharmed, Horath, unless…" he said with a sudden and severe look pointed directly at Horath, "… you seek to incur my wrath."

The overbearing Horath was instantly cowed.

"Please, no, Jor-Taq," he wheedled. "You know I am loyal to you. Have I not proven myself a hundred times over?"

"That is better," Jor-Taq replied with a casual imperiousness.

"Now, Grae-Don, you may release my servant," he said.

And so I did. I gave his heel a push with my hands, and Horath fell flat upon his back.

"I have uses for you, you who call yourself Grae-Don," Jor-Taq said. "Those uses shall become manifest, in time. For now, you shall submit yourself to the gentle teachings of my most loyal servant, Horath. Do you understand?"

I understood that Horath's instructions would be anything but 'gentle', but I kept my silence on that point. All I said to Jor-Taq was, "I understand."

"Now, Horath," Jor-Taq continued. "You shall take this Grae-Don under

[1] Kra – excrement. AG

your tutelage, and teach him well. Enough of the soft teachings of women for this one. Make of him a man."

"Yes, Jor-Taq. I shall do as you say…"

"'Shall'?" Jor-Taq instantly challenged. "'Shall'? Is it not your will to do as I command you?"

"I have no will but yours, Jor-Taq," Horath humbly replied. But I could see, by the sidelong glance he threw at me as he said those words that he said what he needed to say, to Jor-Taq's face. When Jor-Taq was not present, Horath did indeed have a will of his own. And it was his will to ensure that my days ahead were not to be pleasant, not at all.

AFTER OUR audience with Jor-Taq, Horath brought me to another part of the old man's huge and fortress-like residence. This was a room where Jor-Taq's guards dwelt. All of them slept together in a single cavernous hall of bare walls and hard stone floor. The room offered no comforts to the eye or the body – all slept on the floor, with naught but a single sleeping blanket that was issued to each of them.

Every wealthy man has his own private guard, for who will offer him protection, if he does not protect himself? Every wealthy man in Pella'mir fears all others, for he has that which others seek – and it is this fear that keeps many men poor, that they may not attract the attention of burglars and murderers.

All of them fear assassination, some of them obsessively so, and all of them have, among their guards, those who

59

they specially train in the art of assassination.

But some men crave wealth more than they fear death, and so these men provide for themselves guards who they pay to protect them from those who would do them harm.

These guards also keep order generally through the city of Pella'mir, for the wealthy men of the city know that they could not thrive if their world was unsound. So it is left up to them to mete out whatever justice was needed among the citizens of Pella'mir. Since the justice of the guards is usually short and brutal, and dealt without any regard to the well-being of those who receive it, the citizens of Pella'mir seek to avoid any contact with this justice, and so they are generally very well-behaved.

Any minor problems that arise between them, they keep minor. It profits no one to make a small problem great, and so Pella'mir is a generally happy city.

There are a number of wealthy men in Pella'mir, such as Jor-Taq, some who have joined together to form partnerships, the better to protect themselves, not only from the dissatisfaction of the poor, who outnumber them by orders of magnitude, but also from each other, who they each fear more than the poor.

Jor-Taq did not join any of these partnerships. He lived in isolation from all others, almost never leaving his great house, and spending all his days in his study, pursuing his researches with a fanaticism, I would learn, that drove all other thoughts from his mind

– save alone for his fear of assassination. He was also the wealthiest man in Pella'mir, and the most hated. And so his obsessive fear of assassination was not without foundation. Even his own guards despised him. Though they took their payment from him, none of them, not one, felt any true loyalty to the old man.

JOR-TAQ'S guards were hard men, cold men. They had no need for comfort, held it in contempt, and lived with a cult of pain. For pastimes, when they were not on duty, they played games with their knives upon their bodies, to build their endurance.

In one such game, one guard laid his hand upon the floor, fingers splayed, while another thrust the point of his knife between the splayed fingers, one after another, in rapid succession. Sometimes the guard with the knife missed and sliced off a fingertip. Each time a fingertip happened to get sliced off, all those in the room watching burst out into roars of laughter, including he who lost the digit. Losing a finger in this exercise was considered a point of honour among these guards. I saw this game played almost constantly.

In another such game, one guard laid his hand upon the wall, fingers once again splayed, while others threw knives at his outstretched hand, to see who could hit the wall closest to the fingers. Wagers were placed upon these tournaments, and many days' pay was often lost in an instant.

These were hard men, as I say. Brutal men, but, unlike Horath, they were, for the most part, honest men, and honourable.

They practiced a form of scarification that was ritualistic among them, decorating their bodies with welts and scars that described complicated circles and spirals. In some cases, they opened the flesh of their bodies and placed metal beads under their skin, creating rows of bumps in patterns that indicated their rank and accomplishments.

Each part of the body, I learned, had a special significance among them. Arms and hands were devoted to recording feats of the individual. On their chests, they stitched patterns that gave display to their rank and to whose house it was they served. Their backs and legs were given over to symbols that indicated their family and genealogy. By means of these symbols, one could literally read a man, learn from his body who he was, who he served, and what he had done.

These symbols were matters of great honour among them. No man could scar his body alone. It had to always be done with great ceremony, even the least scar, with many witnesses to attest that the scar was deserved, and had been either earned or rightly inherited.

When Horath ushered me into the hall, a dozen of the off-duty guards surrounded us. Horath, the leader of the guard, barked out his orders.

"Take this one in hand, and teach him well. Jor-Taq demands it."

And then he spun on his heel and left me to the kind mercies of the brutal guard. Now my education took a different, harsher, turn. Gone were those happy moments with Shala and Haia, when learning to speak and to read was accompanied with games and treats.

Punishment became the impetus. When I did poorly, my teachers punished me harshly. When I did well, they rewarded me with light punishments.

Every morning, Horath himself awoke me with a kick in the ribs, which provoked great rounds of laughter from the guards. And all through the day, they took turns cuffing and punching me, as they set me to my various tasks.

In addition to my regular duties, they put me to a regimen of exercises to toughen me up; running in place, and climbing ropes, pulling myself up on a bar set into a frame, and squatting and thrusting and pushing and climbing.

I took to it, as I had set it in my heart to kill Horath, and knew that my slight frame would be nothing against his. I must make myself bulky, and hard, like stone, to challenge him. So I endured the cuffing and the punching with as good a spirit as I could muster, knowing that every punch, every slap only made me tougher and stronger than before.

"Half of the fight, boy," one of the guards explained to me, "Is stamina. If you can take more pain than your opponent can give, then you've won." And then he banged the back of my head with his fist to emphasize his point.

Those words have stayed with me, for I have seen it often, since, that a man will provoke a fight, expecting no resistance, but instantly falls to crying like a baby girl, when once he gets the fight he was looking for.

Only but endure – you need not even be able to throw a punch, to make a coward cringe, to recoil in fear. And most men, I have learned, are cowards.

I took the punches, as I say, with as good a spirit as I could muster, but after a time, I had had enough. One evening after I'd been at chores all day, and was sore, and tired, one of the guards shouted at me to clean his muddy sandals for him. I called him a stinking koraph, and told him to do it himself.

He came at me in a rush and a rage, with his fists upraised, bellowing that he was about to give me the beating of my life.

Without thinking, I swung my fist at him, just as he came within striking distance, and hit him fairly on the chin. His head snapped back, with a look of astonishment on his face that I will never forget, and then I quickly followed that punch with two more to the belly.

The wind went out of him and his face went white. He dropped to his knees, hunched over and clutching his stomach. I brought my own knee forward quickly, and kicked him twice in the face, and he fell sprawling backward.

Such a commotion! The instant my antagonist fell on the floor, the guards who saw the short-lived fight between

us filled the hall with their laughter and loud applause.

"It's about time you showed us some spunk!" I heard several say.

"Good job!"

"Well done. You did him right and good!"

The guard I felled to the floor picked himself up, and I was astonished to see him laughing, through bloodied lips and broken nose.

"Haw! Haw! Haw!" he said. "Did you see that? I'm the one who taught him that trick!"

And they all crowded around me, slapping me on the back and generally congratulating me.

Now their attitude toward me changed. They still cuffed and punched me, as before, but now they ducked quickly away as I swung back at them.

From this point on, they included boxing and wrestling in my education – I found that I preferred the boxing, but realized that wrestling was a needful skill, so I strove to excel in that, as well.

After I had gained some mastery in these two skills, two of them, one called Brekkex, and the other, Koax, took it upon themselves to teach me the use of the knife and of the sword. Brekkex taught me how to use the knife. Koax, the sword.

The knives are various. Some are short and straight, some are long and curved. Some come to a point at the tip, some have tips that are curved upward from the cutting edge, some have serrated edges, and some have two, rather than one cutting edge. Some have handles with finger grips, some with holes in the handles for the fingers to fit into. Some have guards between the handle and the blade, and some do not. Each has its own use, I learned, and I was to become proficient in all of them, before my education was to be considered complete.

The swords they use are rather short, with thick, slightly curved blades. They do not come to a point, as I have since seen in other swords, but are cut straight at the end, with a blunt tip. These are brutal weapons that can sometimes be used as clubs. They have only one cutting edge, the opposite edge being thick enough to crack a skull, if necessary.

The two men who undertook to teach me the use of these tools were both excellent teachers, who were patient, when needed, but not too patient. As I first bumbled with the use of these things, they warned me to take care, lest I cut my own head off.

"And you'd be no good then," they said.

But, as I gained in skill, as practiced against them, in sword and knife fighting, they were quick and merciless in taking advantage of any opening, however small, I gave them. So in short time, my body was covered with innumerable scratches, cuts and scars from our practices.

And in the end, we three became rather close friends, especially when I managed to slip in a point of my dagger, and gouge a bit of flesh from them, myself.

"They called you a slow learner, boy," Koax laughed in his loud way. "But I'll be damned if you're not picking it up 'most as fast as I did."

THERE WAS a rigid hierarchy among Jor-Taq's guards. Those who I was quartered with here were among the lowest ranks. They guarded the house and its walls, and were never permitted to the higher floors where Jor-Taq lived. Most of them had never even laid eyes on the old man, but had been recruited into his service by low-ranking guards, themselves.

Somewhat higher in rank were those guards who were permitted to go outside and into the streets of Pella'mir, especially in the neighbourhoods surrounding Jor-Taq's house. Higher in rank than these were Jor-Taq's spies, who infiltrated the guards and houses of the other men of wealth in Pella'mir. Highest in rank and fewest in number were Jor-Taq's assassins, of whom Horath was the chief.

I learned from Brekkex and Koax, and the others among the guards with whom I had established a rough kind of friendship, that Horath was heartily despised by all who knew him. Even Jor-Taq himself, it was rumoured, had grown sick of the man and his overbearing ways.

"I am Jor-Taq's assassin," he proclaimed loudly, to all who would hear, "And I can do whatever I want!"

Whatever he wanted to do was usually to bring misery and suffering to anyone he could. He strode through the streets of Pella'mir, bullying and fighting, and taking what he wanted without paying, daring anyone to challenge him. None did, and the discontent he caused was coming to be so large that even the great Jor-Taq, isolated in his studies away from all humanity, could not ignore it.

SO IT was that one morning, as Brekkex and Koax were teaching me how to hurl a sword – a nice piece of work that requires strong muscles in the forearm, great coordination of hand and eye, and a delicate feel for the weight of the blade, to give it the proper rotation in the air, so that it hits its target fairly – Horath came into the hall with his usual strident bellowing.

"Where is that koraph Grae-don?"

"Right here!" I answered, loudly, and with a touch of brashness I knew would annoy the man.

"Jor-Taq demands to see you, now!" he shouted at me. The man always looked upon the world with a smouldering anger in his eyes, but this day, I sensed, he glared at me with something more than his usual, generalized rage. Now, for some reason, it was me, in particular, that he hated.

"Yes, Horath," I answered. It was terribly impudent of me to address the man by name. Properly, a lower-ranking guard should address a higher-ranking guard only by his title. It was impudent of me to address him at all, for I was the lowest-ranking of all, and properly, should not have uttered even a sound in the presence of the great assassin, but only silently obey his every whim.

He lashed out to give me a clout upon the head for my impudence but I was too quick for him. Before his fist came near me, I raised my sword so that it was in the path of his blow, and he smacked the flat of it dead on with his hand. Knuckles bruised and skin torn, he let loose a howl of pain and rage.

"You will die for that!" he bawled, as the guards in the hall laughed at his discomfiture.

"And you will keep the mighty Jor-Taq waiting, upon your own pleasure?" I taunted him, and loudly enough so that all could hear.

The bullying Horath looked quickly about, seeing that all eyes were upon him. Outnumbered by those who hated him, the assassin was quickly cowed.

"Come with me," he blustered. "Jor-Taq will deal with your insubordination."

"Yes, Horath," I twitted him, again.

"Fare-thee-well, Horath," heckled another guard.

"Good-bye-e-e, Horath," called out another, affecting a high-pitched, mincing tone.

"Toodle-oooo, Horath."

And so Horath ushered me out of the hall to a chorus of ridicule and laughter, his face burning with stifled rage. He would have killed me on the spot, I knew, had not Jor-Taq demanded to see me. I would live that long, at least, but I knew that Horath would not let me live longer than Jor-Taq required me.

And so ended my education among the guards of Jor-Taq. I would see my friends of the guards only once again, in the days to come, under extremely altered circumstances, and many would be the times that I am grateful to Brekkex and Koax for their brief, but very timely, friendship.

CONTINUES NEXT WEEK

Copyright © Gregory KH Bryant 2013

ABOUT THE AUTHOR

Gregory K. H. Bryant is an author and artist residing in Falls Church, Virginia, in the United States. His poetry, short stories and screen plays have appeared widely in the small and underground presses for over twenty years. Currently he oversees the digitization of historical records with the Office of the Registrar, National Air and Space Museum, Smithsonian Institution, where he has been on staff since 1978.

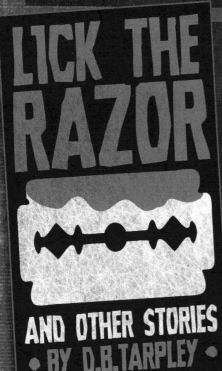